MR. DE LUCA'S HORSE

by Marjorie Paradis

Illustrated by Judith Brown

Most boys have some money problems, but Brett's were somewhat different. His Mother was ill in England and he and his artist father were trying to keep house while Brett's father taught and Brett went to High School. He had promised to buy his mother a mixing machine, but he had also told Mr. De Luca, the junk man, that he would not only buy his old broken-down horse, but also his wagon. Needing money desperately made Brett a very busy boy. He sold old newspapers to the junk dealer, worked on a merry-go-round at Coney Island on Saturdays, and modeled for painters and advertisements while he studied at night. His main problem was where he was going to keep the horse when Mr. De Luca sold it to him, a problem he had neglected to mention to his father. His adventures are fun, and he learns a lot about people and finds a new appreciation for his parents when they are reunited.

* * * *

Classification and Dewey Decimal: Fiction (Fic)

About the Author:

MARJORIE PARADIS's affection for her home town, New York City, prompted, in part at least, the writing of this book. In her city she attended high school and then Columbia University, and began her writing career. She has written adult novels, plays, one movie, a great many short stories and books for children. In addition to writing Mrs. Paradis enjoys golf, gardening, rug hooking, and oil painting. She and her husband, Adrian, have made several trips to Europe and Mexico.

About the Illustrator:

A serious illustrator of children's books, JUDITH BROWN spends most of her time working at her art. Of the 14 books she has illustrated, two of them were also written by her. Born in New York City, she was graduated from New York University and also attended Cooper Union and the Parsons School of Design.

DRAWINGS BY JUDITH BROWN

Marjorie Paradis

Mr. De Luca's Horse

1967 FIRST CADMUS EDITION
THIS SPECIAL EDITION IS PUBLISHED BY ARRANGEMENT WITH
THE PUBLISHERS OF THE REGULAR EDITION
ATHENEUM PUBLISHERS
BY

E. M. HALE AND COMPANY
EAU CLAIRE, WISCONSIN

This edition lithographed in U. S. A. by Wetzel Bros., Inc., Milwaukee 2, Wisconsin

To JOEL PARADIS *who is also a horse lover*

*C*hapters

Mr. De Luca's Horse

Driving

At the first click of the dismissal bell, Brett picked up his brief case, dashed into the coat room, grabbed his windbreaker and, ignoring all rules, took the stairs two at a time. He had a date with Mr. De Luca and he didn't want to be late.

Seeing his father in the hall below, he slowed his pace. It was a nuisance, sometimes, having his father teach art in the same school.

"Hi! Dad." Brett tried to hide his impatience. "What can I do for you?" Although tall for his age, he had to tilt his head to look into his father's eyes, for Warner Barnes stood six feet three.

"It's about the Velskin commission, B. B. I just phoned—"

"Could you tell me out on the steps, Dad? I'm expecting Mr. De Luca."

His father gave a little chuckle and said, as he led the way, "You're an optimist to expect his poor old nag to amble this far."

Brett, tightening his lips, wondered how his father, usually so kind, could be so cruel about Jerry. The answer was: he didn't love horses. He said he didn't. He said he preferred dogs.

Out on the school steps, one glance along the curb relieved Brett's mind. Thank goodness he had beaten Mr. De Luca.

"Yes, Dad, you were saying?"

"I was about to say that Velskin likes my portfolio, and they want to see me this afternoon."

"Well good for them. Are they ready to sign you up?"

"Hardly, B. B. It's a big campaign. Biggest deal I ever touched. Ten, twelve thousand, and, best of all, there'd be plenty of time so it wouldn't interfere with my teaching."

"Gee, Dad, gee! If you land it, will you up my allowance? Make it the same as George's?"

"I might, at least for the year. Know what he gets?"

Brett nodded. "It's five times as much."

His father didn't even wince. "If I get the commission, you'll get your five dollars a week. Meanwhile, on your way home, buy a couple of frozen chicken pies and some dessert. I'll be late." He handed Brett some bills from a lean wallet, gave a farewell salute, and ducked back into the school, leaving Brett in a golden haze.

Five dollars a week! And his father *might* get the commission. He ought to. He was a good artist. What would life be like with such an allowance? Since last November, over four months ago, he'd been saving, and scrinching, and going without everything to buy his mother a present. Adding his allowance and what he made by selling old newspapers he had saved a total of only $18.40, but with his new allowance, think how it would mount up!

He descended the steps slowly, his thoughts too fragile to be jarred. A thump on his back awakened him from his daydream and, turning, he saw George Clayton.

"Been looking for you, you old good for nothing," said George.

Ever since George had entered Cluett in September, and especially since Brett's mother had gone to England, the two boys had been boon companions. George loved Brett's studio-life, and Brett was drawn to George because he knew so much about horses. Not only did he own one, but his uncle, up in the country near their summer home, had a big riding academy.

"Say, George, I was just wondering, what does a horse cost?"

"A race horse, like you're always talking about? I'd guess $10,000—maybe more."

"No, I mean just a nice saddle horse."

"I don't know. A couple of hundred bucks, I suppose. Why?"

Brett shrugged. "Maybe sometime if Dad buys that house in Yonkers, I can own one."

"Ah, heck, don't talk about moving. You'd never get anything as wonderful as that studio. Look, Martin's coming for me today. Want a hitch?"

"No, thanks, I'm getting one."

"You don't mean with—"

"I mean Mr. De Luca."

"But, B. B., wouldn't you rather go with *me* than *him*?"

"If you're asking do I like you better than him, of course I do. You're my best friend; he's more of a business acquaintance. But I'd rather ride with him because I prefer horses to cars."

George gave an unpleasant chuckle. "Call *that* a horse?"

"Just a minute, George. I don't make fun of your car."

"How could you? What's better than a Cadillac?"

"A Mercedes Benz and lots of European cars, but I'm not running down your limousine so don't you run down Jerry."

George shrugged good-naturedly. "O.K., O.K."

The boys drifted down to the curb to wait.

"I was just thinking, Brett, Friday we're going to the country for our first week end. Want to come?"

Brett looked at George in wide-eyed amazement. Did he want to come? What a silly question. Hadn't he dreamed about it all winter! "Sure I want to. Of course. What do you think?"

"I think it's too cold, but with you along it won't be so bad."

"And will I visit your uncle's riding academy?"

"If the weather's decent."

"You said you'd teach me to ride your horse."

"Sure I will. Nothing to it. Ask your father if you

can come, and I'll speak to my mother. There's old Martin. See you tomorrow."

George leaped into a black limousine and slammed the door. The boys made faces at each other through the window as the car slid away.

A moment later Brett heard the jangle of discordant bells. He stood eagerly at the curb as a flat junk cart drew up.

Along the side of the wagon in yellow, uneven lettering, were the words: MERCHANDISE BOUGHT AND SOLD MR. DE LUCA PROP.

The merchandise today included several bundles of newspapers—some of which Brett had sold to Mr. De Luca that morning—a bag of rags, a rusty gas stove, and a refrigerator lying on its side. The Prop, Mr. De Luca, a small man with an overdue shave and a long mustache, sat hunched in the driver's seat. The reins lay slack in one hand, an ancient whip in the other, its stubby end resting on Jerry's spine.

"Hi, Mr. De Luca," Brett called, pausing to pat Jerry. His fingers left an imprint on the dusty hide. He really is old, thought Brett, as he offered some sugar on an open palm. He envisioned the horse he would buy, young and frisky—a Palomino perhaps.

Jerry slobbered as he crunched the sugar; and Brett thought that his bloodshot eyes, gazing through drooping lids, looked unusually sad, as if he had read Brett's thoughts.

"You're all right, Jerry, you sure are." He said it aloud for anyone to hear, and drew a deep breath of the pungent odor. Whatever anyone said about Jerry, no one could deny that he smelled like a horse.

Wiping his palm on his pants, Brett picked up his brief case, tossed it into the wagon, and scrambled up beside Mr. De Luca.

"Would you like-a, mebby to drive?" asked the Prop.

"Could I *really*?" Brett doubted his ears. This was the third time Mr. De Luca had given him a ride, but never had he made an offer like this.

"What I say, I mean," answered the Prop, shifting along the seat and letting Brett scramble over his thin legs.

"Thanks ever and ever so much," Brett said, taking the proffered reins.

"Don't-a be showin' off and try to go fast. Keep-a near the curb. Here, hold the whip."

Brett did as he was directed. He shook the reins and clucked but not a bell swayed.

With a sudden yank at the reins, Mr. De Luca roared in a voice of thunder, "Git-up!"

Jerry twitched an ear, took a slow step, another step. The bells swayed until they jangled. They were off.

Figuring

"You like-a drive?" Mr. De Luca asked sharply. He always spoke as if he had just been insulted, but Brett was used to it.

"I love it, Mr. De Luca. You're awfully good to let me."

Mr. De Luca took a half-smoked cigar from his pocket and lighted it with difficulty. "I don't-a mind, just so you don't do nothing crazy."

A stream of honking cars swept around the junk cart, but they disturbed neither Brett nor the Prop—nor Jerry, for that matter.

"Friday I'm going to the country with a friend who'll teach me to ride horseback," boasted Brett. Nothing ever impressed Mr. De Luca, but he had to share his good news.

"Waste o' time. Horses—they is done for."

Although prepared for some objection, this statement, more outrageous than anything his father had ever said, came as a shock.

"They'll *never* be done for, Mr. De Luca. Maybe there won't be so many *work* horses, but there'll always be race horses. My grandfather in Surrey, England, used to breed race horses. I was born near Epsom Downs, the best race track in the world."

"So that's-a why you talk fancy, because you're-a English."

As always, when people spoke of his English accent, Brett felt annoyed. It seemed to him that he talked like any other boy.

"No, Mr. De Luca, I'm not English. I'm an American like my father. So's my mother, now. I'm no different from any of the other kids."

"Me—I'm American, too." Mr. De Luca puffed proudly on his cigar butt. "I'm Italian-born. You're English-born. That makes us different. Some-a people think I'm more dumber than them because I don't talk so good, but they only know one language and me—I speak-a two. Don't be a-mindin' that you're different. Everybody is different from everybody—and that's the way they're meant to be."

Brett considered this statement and found comfort in it. Maybe his father had a right to prefer dogs to horses.

"Yes, Mr. De Luca, I guess that's so." With the least pull on the reins, he halted Jerry for a red light.

"What people don't like," continued Mr. De Luca, "is when you're better than them, as f'instance me talkin'-a two languages and you bein' more politer."

"You think I'm polite!" Brett was amazed.

"And so-a you are," insisted Mr. De Luca. "Take that Mister stuff. To everybody else I'm-a Joe, and you

can-a call me Joe, too, if you want; but the way you-a
say my name sounds sort of—not-a bad."

"Then I'll go right on calling you Mr. De Luca.
If I really am polite, it's because of my mother; and
my father says I ought to keep in practice so she won't
be disappointed when she gets home."

"Your Ma away?"

"Yes, since the tenth of November." Brett stared
at Jerry's bony back.

"And you no-a see her none?"

"Too far. England."

"It's not none of my business—" Mr. De Luca
interrupted himself to relight his cigar, "but-a why she
go so far for so long?"

"To get cured," Brett said, proud of his firm voice.

"Cured o' what?"

"She—she was sick all summer, then she had
pneumonia." His fingers tightened on the reins. "When
she got better, they discovered she had something else
—something worse." He didn't attempt to say the
awful word.

"Tuber-colosis?" asked Mr. De Luca.

Brett nodded.

"And there wasn't no place near by where she
could-a gone?"

"Oh, yes, lots of them," Brett said soberly. "But
they cost too much, especially when her uncle has one
of the best sanitariums in the whole world and he invited her to come as his guest."

Mr. De Luca nodded. "When-a you save money

you gotter pay with-a somethin' else. Your poor papa must-a be lonely."

"Lonely, my father? Anything but," Brett said scornfully. "He has stacks of friends. Ever since my mother's been away, he's always going places with them or they're coming to see him. Don't worry about him. He knows how to have a good time." Brett realized that his voice sounded sharp, and he hadn't meant to criticize his father. "He's jolly and that makes him popular," the boy explained more quietly. "I'm sure he must miss Mom an awful lot, but he says worry doesn't help."

"Worry don't help tuber-colosis none," agreed Mr. De Luca. "Some gets well and some don't."

"Well, my mother's almost cured now," Brett said, wanting to believe it. "Green light, Jerry, giddap."

The horse remained motionless save for a twitching ear.

"Git up," roared Mr. De Luca, yanking at the reins. "Sometimes I tink he is-a dead on his feet."

"Maybe you expect too much," Brett said severely. "After all, he isn't exactly young, and he's had a long day."

"He make-a my day long," complained Mr. De Luca.

"Is he very old?" Brett asked in an undertone. His mother had taught him that elderly people did not like to discuss their ages. Maybe animals felt the same.

Mr. De Luca, however, had no regard for Jerry's feelings. "Too old," he said loud and clear. "I have me a friend with a small truck, who-a very sick. He still work—ice—but he very sick all the same. Maybe I buy his auto when he quit."

"But not soon, I hope, Mr. De Luca."

"Who can-a tell? He looks more worse every day, that I can see. Remember, it is good business to look ahead."

"I am looking ahead," Brett said pridefully. "My father's buying a house in Yonkers as soon as the title's cleared, and I don't want you to give up Jerry until after we move in June."

"What-a for you move to the country?" scolded Mr. De Luca. "I try to teach you business. Business is here in the city."

"We have to move on account of—you know—my mother. She'll be home in August."

"Oh, that," agreed Mr. De Luca grudgingly. "But you don't *want* to go, do you?"

"I'll be glad in one way," Brett said truthfully. "There's a wonderful barn on the place, and if my father gets a big commission, I'd save for—" He paused, remembering that Mr. De Luca cared less for horses than his father. "I could save for a pedigreed Newfoundland dog. But I'll miss you an awful lot, Mr. De Luca."

He would, however, miss Jerry even more, especially now that he was allowed to drive. He looked sadly at the animal's bony back, the knobby spine, the curved ribs so pitifully visible under the hide. Poor, dear Jerry.

Regretfully he drew up at the corner of Second Avenue and 25th Street, dropped the ancient whip into the socket, and handed the reins over to the Prop.

"I'm getting off here. Have to go to the store on the way home."

"Want-a I call for you tomorrow?"

"Of course. Every day."

"Who can-a say every day? But tomorrow—yes."

"Thanks a lot," Brett said jumping down. He reached for his brief case and, ignoring a variety of impatient horns, paused to pat the horse's neck. " 'Bye, Jerry. 'Bye, Mr. De Luca. Thanks again."

He waited until Jerry ambled off, then hurried down the street, well knowing he would pass his favorite store, Harrison's, Limited, the British Equestrian Shop. For years, ever since he had lived in America, the store had fascinated him. Before he was old enough to go to school, he and his mother, who loved horses, too, had come every day to gaze at the stuffed Palomino that stood in one of the double windows. Brett slowed his steps as he neared the store. Nowhere else did his mother seem quite as close. The one thing that always comforted him was the thought of the wonderful homecoming present he would give her. That raw November afternoon as she gave a final wave before disappearing into the transatlantic plane, the idea had popped into his mind like an inspiration. He would save and buy her an electric beater. She had wanted one for a long time and had even picked out the make. An Acme.

Abreast of the store he paused, as always, to ad-

mire the Palomino's pale tan hide, the flowing white
mane and tail, but today it possessed an even greater
fascination. Who could tell? Maybe one year from this
very moment he, Brett Barnes, would own a horse exactly like the one in the window! The thought filled
him with an almost unbearable joy.

He stopped at the delicatessen store for the two
frozen chicken pies and, for dessert, a small apple pie.
Then he went out of his way to look at the Acme beater
displayed in the window of an electric appliance store.

Anticipating his increased allowance, he went into
the store and asked the clerk if they ever had special
sales of Acme beaters.

"Not *Acme*," said the salesman in a shocked tone.
"We have a more reasonable make that—"

"Oh, no," interrupted Brett. He wasn't going to
short-change his mother.

Retracing his steps, he turned down his own street.
His home was the second floor of a low brick building
that had once been a garage. It crouched between two
towering apartment houses.

Silently unlocking the front door, he crept up
the steep stairs, anxious to escape Mrs. McCray, who,
with her husband, Hugh McCray, a sculptor, occupied the other apartment.

It made a strange home, this one vast room with
three windows back and front as well as a skylight. The
jog beyond the stairs had been partitioned off to make
a small bath and a fair-sized kitchen. An area, including two of the front windows, had been blocked off,

making a cubicle for Brett. The rest of the studio, with its grand piano, two couches, a dining table that could be extended to seat twelve, a grandfather's clock, an artist's table and numerous chairs served as bedroom, dining room, living room, and studio.

Along one wall hung some of his father's oil paintings, along another his mother's water colors; for she, too, was an artist.

Kicking the door closed behind him, Brett went into his cubicle, flung his brief case on his desk, dropped the pies on his bed, and began to figure on a slip of paper.

He needed a little over six dollars more to pay for the Acme. With an allowance of five dollars a week plus fifty cents for the newspapers he sold each Monday to Mr. De Luca, he'd have an income of $5.50 a week.

He multiplied quickly and the result stunned him.

Enough and more than enough. In one year he could own a horse!

What a glorious future! This week end he would learn to ride horseback. In June he would have a stable. In August his mother would return. And next spring he would own a horse.

Joy tingled in his veins as he gazed at the figures before him. Too excited to sit, he jumped up, looked at the clock, and remembered his obligation. Soon after he had popped the chicken pies into the oven and lighted it, his father returned.

"Hi, Dad, did they sign on the dotted line?"

"Give them time, boy; give them time."

"But you will get it, don't you think, Dad? You're a good artist, everybody says so. They like your portfolio, so why shouldn't you get it?"

"For a thousand good reasons. There are at least that many other good artists in this city. Suppose we try not to think about it, B. B."

"O.K., Dad," agreed Brett, knowing that his father asked the impossible. "Say, George has invited me to his country home for the week end. Can I go?"

His father's worried expression gave way to his usual lightheartedness.

"That would be fine, B. B. He's a nice kid. Funny thing, I've been invited to a museum opening in Philadelphia. With you taken care of, I might go."

"You could have gone and left me," Brett said, realizing how often he must be a nuisance.

"I could, I suppose, but it works out better this way. How's your blue suit?"

"Dad, don't be crazy. Dungarees are all I'll need."

"I'll iron a pair of your pajamas. Your mother wouldn't want you to take them rough dry," his father said thoughtfully. "Got a decent pair?"

Brett shook his head.

"Better buy some—save me a pressing job. What do I smell?"

"Golly, the chicken pies!"

They dashed into the kitchen and Mr. Barnes yanked open the oven door.

"Done to a turn. B. B. You're quite a cook."

The Bargain

BRETT left for school later than he should the next morning and ran the nine blocks, slipping into his classroom just before the bell. Panting for breath, he caught George's eye, pointed to himself, and nodded.

This, he thought, stated as clearly as words that the week end was all right for him; but George scowled, shook his head, and shrugged. He didn't seem to understand the gesture.

It was noon and the two boys were eating in the school dining room before Brett had an opportunity to explain what he had meant.

"Look, can't you understand anything? I was telling you it's okay about Friday. My father says I can go."

"Oh, that." George forked his goulash as if he were looking for a hidden treasure. "Well—er—Mom —I mean—you know, I said I'd ask her."

Brett nodded. "And she doesn't want me?"

"Sure she wants you. Of course she does. That part's all right. She likes you a lot. She thinks you talk like the Duke of Windsor, whoever he is. But it's just—

just—I'm not taking anyone." Under his breath he added, "She makes me sick." Brett thought he said she was sick.

"I understand, George. You've got to have a lot of patience when a person's sick."

"My mother's not sick. She's crazy scared of bugs; germs and bugs."

"You mean on account of my mother? But she's been gone five months!"

"No, it's not your mother. It's just—"

"Just what?"

"It's the junk man. Like a ninny I happened to say you liked to ride with a junk man and *that* did it. She says anyone who rides with a junk man will bring home bugs."

"I don't. I never brought a bug home in all my life."

"That's what I told her, but she says how would you know."

"I guess my father would know pretty quick."

George nodded. "Don't take it out on me, B. B. That's exactly what I said."

"Then what did she say?"

George shrugged and again went prospecting in his goulash.

"She must have said something," insisted Brett.

"Sure she did."

"What was it?"

"Something about artists not caring if they did have bugs."

"That's a lie." Brett sprang to his feet, pushing the chair over backwards.

"Brett!" called Miss Simpson in charge of the dining room. "Apologize to George."

"It wasn't him told the lie," Brett mumbled.

"Then calm down and finish your dinner."

Under her stern gaze he straightened the chair and seated himself, but he opened his mouth neither to eat nor speak.

"Look, Brett, don't get mad at me," begged George. "Maybe if you'd quit going with the junk man —" He ate a roll as he waited for the suggestion to sink in, then driven by impatience he added in a muffled voice, "you do that, and I'll ask her again."

"I will *not*." Brett made a hissing noise of contempt. "And what's more, I wouldn't touch your mother with a ten-foot pole." He said it as if he were depriving George's mother of a rare treat.

Without waiting for custard, which he hated, he got up, carefully this time, obtained permission from Miss Simpson to leave the room, and went into the gym.

He sent a ball in a slow curve against the wall. It bounced wearily and rolled to his feet where he looked at it without picking it up. So artists didn't know when they had bugs! The nerve of that woman! His mother was an artist, too, and nobody ever lived who was cleaner than his mother. Even now, didn't his father have Mrs. Haggerty every week?

Picking up the ball he slammed it at the wall, and let it bounce itself out as a new thought possessed him.

What about his father's week end? Would he feel he had
to give up his trip? Brett wondered how many such
jaunts he had already refused.

Suppose he wasn't told. Suppose Brett even packed
his suitcase Friday morning as if he were going. It
wouldn't be telling an untruth. The idea pleased him.
A week end all alone could be quite exciting.

That afternoon he hurried out of school ahead of
George and found Mr. De Luca directly in front of the
door, dividing the line of waiting cars.

"Hey, you, get along," called one of the drivers.

"I sit-a good here," Mr. De Luca answered sternly.

Brett, with deliberate slowness, fed Jerry a raw
carrot and three lumps of sugar, one at a time.

Climbing into the driver's seat, he caught George's
pleading gaze, but, stony-faced, he reached for the
whip. Mr. De Luca bawled his order, and they jogged
off.

"Does Jerry have a nice stall?" asked Brett, fearful
lest the horse had lost weight since yesterday.

"All-a right," answered Mr. De Luca and, reaching between the buttons of his shirt, scratched himself
noisily.

"If I knew where you kept him, Mr. De Luca, I'd
be glad to help you with him."

"No, no," discouraged the owner. "I can't-a be
bothered with you all the time." And again he scratched
himself.

Brett wondered uncomfortably if George's mother
might be right.

"I hope your sick friend is better," he said to hide his embarrassment.

"He ain't. He's bad. Maybe I get the auto sooner than I think."

Brett had a sudden idea. Even if his father got the commission it would be at least a year before he had enough to buy a real horse—that is, a young horse.

"Would you say, Mr. De Luca, that Jerry's awfully valuable?"

"He's got-a value, all right. Some. Not too much."

"If it's all right for me to ask, how much do you expect to get for him?"

"Twenty-five-a dollar. Not a cent less."

Brett sat stunned by the price. Only twenty-five dollars! Why, he had almost that much already. Of course his money was for the Acme, but he'd still have four months in which to save and with a chance of a BIG allowance this was no problem at all.

A horse for twenty-five dollars!

He drew a breath of sheer joy. "When you're ready to sell, Mr. De Luca, please give me first chance."

"You? Where-a you keep him?"

"I told you we're buying a house with a barn, and the barn has three stalls."

"Maybe your papa wouldn't want you to buy a horse, that is—a—is a horse like Jerry."

This was a question Brett refused to consider and he brushed it aside with a wave of the whip. "Any father would be proud to have his son buy a horse out of his own money, and my mother would be delighted. Jerry's a very nice horse. A roan, I suppose you'd call him."

"Mebby," agreed Mr. De Luca. "A roan sounds more better than what I call him." And he gave a little chuckle.

Brett's eyes became soft with love as he gazed at Jerry's sagging head that bobbed with each step. He felt a smothering sense of possessiveness. This living, breathing animal would soon be his.

If only his father felt differently about horses. One thing Brett knew for sure: he would say nothing about Jerry until he was bought and paid for.

Adventuring

"I CAN see question marks big as fishhooks in your eyes, B. B.," Warner Barnes said to his son that night at dinner. "About that commission, I mean."

"But, Dad, I haven't said a word."

"You don't need to. Maybe I should say tenterhooks, not fishhooks. The answer is I haven't heard a word; and with each passing minute, even an optimist like me becomes less hopeful."

"I know," Brett said sympathetically, as he felt his dreams dying. "Me, too. I wish I could earn some money." The last was a sudden inspiration.

"I hate to hold you down to such a small allowance when all the other boys have so much," his father commented. "But I seem faced with a mountain of expenses and I'm not as good at finances as your mother. Saving for anything special?"

Brett was ready for the question. "You said if I had a dog, I ought to own a Newfoundland; and they're not cheap." He felt proud of himself. He'd given the wrong impression without actually lying.

"A Newfoundland's a wonderful dog, but probably you'd love a stray from the pound just as much."

"Could be," Brett agreed cheerfully. "Just the same I could use a little extra money. Know anyone who'd give me fifty cents an hour as a model?"

"Since professional models are demanding fifty times as much, there ought to be somebody who could use you. I'll ask around."

"Thanks, Dad." Brett reached over and took the frying pan from the stove. He gave his father half of the potatoes and ate the rest from the skillet.

"B. B., my son, we must improve our manners. Your mother would never eat in the kitchen, and if she could see us now—me with the milk carton and you the frying pan, I fear she'd have a relapse. Yes, we'll have to change our ways."

"But, Dad, we still have lots of time. We might start in June when we get to the country."

His father frowned. "I'll feel a lot better when I hear that the title's cleared."

"You're afraid we might *not* get the place?" Brett gave no thought to the shabby frame house with a narrow porch; his mind was fixed on the barn with the three stalls. "It's just what we want."

"Yes, with imagination and hard work I think we could make something rather nice out of it. I guess that's why I'm anxious. Considering current prices, it's so cheap I'm suspicious."

The next morning Brett felt better about George. He really wasn't to blame, it was his mother; and anyway, soon Brett wouldn't have to depend on George or anyone else for a horse. Big allowance or not, he'd own one of his own. The thought filled him with secret joy.

George was leaving the coat room as Brett entered.

"Save a place for me at lunch, George. I've decided not to be mad."

"Gee, thanks, Brett. I've been feeling awful."

That noon as they were being served, Brett said in an undertone, "Keep this to yourself, I'm not telling anyone, not even my father. He still thinks I'm going with you but the fact is I'm staying home *alone*."

"You are! What'll you do with yourself?"

"Plenty. Friday afternoon I'll go to Coney Island." He made his plans as he talked and Coney Island sounded exciting; also it wouldn't cost much. "Saturday I might take in a ball game. Sunday, of course, I go to Sunday School. Oh, I'll have myself a good time. I can eat at the Automat if I like. I often do when my father has a dinner date. Or maybe I'll cook my own meals. It's going to be a lot of fun."

"It sure will," agreed George enviously. "Gee, B. B., you're lucky. I don't want my mother to be sick or anything, but she sure spoils my fun. I hate going to the country without you."

"You have your horse. You can ride him."

"If you think that's any pleasure, it's because you've never ridden. It's my idea of nothing—nothing at all. Where do you ride? To nowhere and back." George's tone changed and suddenly became wheedling. "I just love your studio, B. B. It's so exciting and—and free. Can't I spend the week end with you, if my mother'll let me?"

"She wouldn't, not any more than she'd let me visit you," Brett said coldly, and George nodded his head in sad agreement.

Thursday night father and son packed their suitcases and Friday morning, before leaving early, Mr. Barnes gave Brett five dollars, together with final instructions.

"Buy George's mother a nice one-pound box of chocolates and see that you don't eat them all. I'll be home Sunday afternoon. If you're going to be later than seven, give me a ring."

"All right, Dad, I will. Thanks." Brett took the bill and hurried to his cubicle feeling very guilty. Before leaving for school he hid his suitcase under his bed, lest his father return unexpectedly. He also tucked the money into a flat tobacco tin, which held his savings, and fitted it into an inner pocket. Not that he expected to spend a cent of it—he had change in another pocket —but when one went adventuring, it was wise to have plenty of money.

Delayed by a special meeting, it was after four when he reached Coney Island. That afternoon the bright spring sunshine had encouraged many concessionaires to open their stands; and as Brett headed for the boardwalk, he heard barkers calling: "Frozen custard! Delicious frozen custard!" "Ride the whirlwind. Thrill of a lifetime." But although he had his savings, the five dollar bill his father had given him, and forty-two cents left from his weekly allowance, he resolutely withstood all temptation.

As he cut down a side street, he caught the glitter of a revolving merry-go-round and heard the thud and blast of the music together with the jingle jangle of bells. How he used to love a merry-go-round! And so did his mother! Funny thing, when you're a kid and would give the world for a brass ring, your arms aren't long enough to reach it.

Once his mother had caught one and given it to him.

Striding west on the boardwalk, the wind blew cold from the ocean and the sun dazzled his vision. Some of the time he walked backward, thinking as he did so, of George's complaint about horseback riding. It didn't make sense when you were galloping on horseback, but it did when you were walking on your own feet. What fun was he having now? Coney Island wasn't at all as he remembered it. The night he'd come with his parents, summer before last, the place had been dazzling with lights and tingling with music and they'd gone on everything. It would be more fun now, he supposed, if he spent a little money.

He was, of course, too old to ride on the merry-go-round, but he could at least buy himself an ice cream cone. Walking with an object put vitality into his stride and he hurriedly retraced his steps looking for an open stand. When he found one, however, he decided it was too chilly to enjoy ice cream. Frozen custard was no better. There was always the merry-go-round, if he wanted to be a kid.

He knew what he'd do. He'd try to get a job there for tomorrow. Head high, shoulders swinging, he hurried on. The distant sound of the organ identified the street and he skipped down the boardwalk steps.

The merry-go-round revolved slowly as he hopped on. He made his way past three glossy steeds to select a Palomino, striding it as it dipped to receive him. Kid stuff this, all right. He knew exactly what kind of machinery made the horses look as if they galloped; even so, and despite his age and height, he loved it!

He heard the snap of a ring yanked from the holder; snap, snap, and snap. The child on the black horse ahead of him touched the ring, but could not pull it out. Brett never missed. He stacked them on his left forefinger. Finally he saw the glitter of the brass ring. The little boy on the black horse leaned over as far as he could but was swept along without success. Brett felt a great gush of pride as he snatched the ring out of the holder. A winner, for the first time in his life!

He tossed the black rings into the waiting basket as his horse slowed its pace. He'd won a free ride.

Poor little kid on the black horse. Brett knew, from years of failure, exactly how he felt.

He slipped off his horse and made his way to the boy.

"I have something for you," he said standing on tiptoe, then bending his knees to accommodate himself to the motion of the horse. "Here," and he gave the child his winning ring.

The clang of a bell had tolled the end of the ride,

and a woman came hurrying over to the little boy. Un-buckling his strap she said angrily, "What's he done?"

An old man in slouchy pants joined them. "Any trouble?"

"No, sir," said Brett, wishing he had kept the brass ring. "This little kid couldn't quite reach the ring. I got it," he held up his prize, "and I was giving it to him. That's all."

"Oh," said the old man, taking the ring himself. "So that's it."

"I don't understand what's going on," said the mother.

"He's giving your kid the brass ring so he can have a free ride. Here's the ticket."

"Oh," said the mother, in a very different tone. "That's what I call nice, very nice indeed. Say 'Thank you', Junior."

But Brett didn't wait to be thanked. He hopped off the platform and made his way to a fat man with a dead cigar clenched between his teeth.

"Excuse me, sir, but are you the owner?"

The man nodded.

"I could work for you tomorrow, if you wanted me."

The man shook his head.

"I'm strong and willing; and I'll work for fifty cents an hour, if you'd change your mind."

The man shifted his cigar to the corner of his mouth.

"Kids what talk fancy like you ain't worth two bits an hour."

"But would you try me if I came?"

The man shrugged. "Always stuff to do in the spring."

"When should I get here?"

"Early, or not at all. I start work at eight."

"I'll be here before that," promised Brett.

Working

BRETT bought two hot dogs festooned with sauerkraut and a cup of frozen custard, which he paid for out of his father's five dollars, wrapping the change in a handkerchief. That was fair enough. He never bought his food out of his allowance.

It was eight o'clock by the time he crept up the studio stairs; but despite his caution, he had no more than closed his door before he heard mounting footsteps and realized the worst had happened.

He knew if he ignored the knock, Mrs. McCray would summon the police. With a sigh he opened the door.

"Brett, you poor boy, what has happened!" Mrs. McCray invariably imagined the worst, and now she radiated sympathy.

"Nothing happened, Mrs. McCray. I just got home, that's all."

"But your father told me you would both be away until Sunday!"

Brett kept his voice as polite as possible. "I know, we were to be, but I changed my plans."

"And you're here alone!"

"Not exactly, you're downstairs."

"When are you expecting your father? Not until Sunday? Tomorrow we go to Bay Ridge to spend the night with my granddaughter, Gladys. Then you *will* be alone."

"I'll be all right." Brett tried to inch the door to, without success.

"I don't believe your father has any idea you've come home." She looked at him sharply, awaiting his answer, but he lowered his eyes and said nothing.

As he gazed at her tapping foot, he had an impulse to step on it good and hard; but he did not move.

"I have an idea, Brett! A wonderful idea! You come with us. Gladys will be delighted."

Brett swallowed. Shrill, stupid, fat Gladys!

"We're leaving tomorrow after lunch, and we'll be home early Sunday." She smiled at him, well pleased with the plan, and released her hold on the door.

Brett took advantage of this opportunity and forced a smile. "Thank you, Mrs. McCray." When the opening was reduced to a mere slot he added, "But I have a job tomorrow." The lock clicked and he called through the closed door, "Thanks again, Mrs. McCray."

If he had been rude he was sorry, but he had done the best he could.

He reached his place of employment fifteen minutes early the next morning and found the carousel boarded tightly, but promptly on the hour he saw his boss swinging across the street.

"So you did come," he said, voicing his surprise. He unlocked a door, and Brett followed him into the gloom of the barricaded area which was, the next instant, ablaze with light.

"My name's Jake," the man said, substituting an old sweater for his jacket. He tossed a heavy green sweater to Brett. "Here, wear this. What's your name?"

"Brett Barnes. I'm called B. B."

"B. B. Buckshot, eh? B. B., you're hired for at least two hours, until we open. If you're any good, I'll keep you on. I like to have the horses washed every year, washed careful. I'll start you on that, and work with you."

He brought a pail of hot water, two sponges, and a quantity of rags and showed Brett how to squeeze the sponge before digging into every crack and crevice.

"Maybe it ain't very excitin', but it's a job as has to be done," Jake said severely. "Now, you take that horse, and I'll take this."

Brett, for his part, found it quite exciting. He enjoyed wiping the bold, bulging eyes, the sleek sides, the raised hoofs. Although the morning was chilly, and despite the fact that the sweater cuff grew sodden, he worked with pleasure heightened by the thought that before too many months he would be currying a real horse.

At ten o'clock he was taken from his job to help remove the boardings. They had finished all but the inside ring of little horses. Jake said that could go until next week, a remark which delighted Brett, for he felt it included him.

By this time the old man had come and so had another man to work the machinery. Soon the glittering carousel was revolving, and thumping music filled the neighborhood. The old man sold tickets and Brett collected them, but neither of them was busy, for few children bought rides. Even so Brett felt very important walking between the horses on the revolving floor. Once he jumped off when the merry-go-round was going too fast, and almost fell.

"None of that kid stuff," growled Jake. "You've got a job, that's what. Either you do it like a grown-up or you git, see?"

Brett was given half an hour for lunch. He bought a duplicate of the previous night's supper. When he returned, to his great delight, Jake let him take charge of the rings, which had not been in operation during the morning. He listened carefully to the instructions and proudly mounted the ladder to his little perch. It was his duty to feed the iron rings into a slot ending with the prize brass ring. The number to be used varied according to the skill of the riders.

He found he could more or less select the winner. As the black rings were snapped out of the extended arm, he tried to judge which rider would most appreciate the free ticket. He felt like Santa Claus sitting on the North Pole.

As the afternoon progressed and the horses were in greater demand, the rides became shorter, so that it was impossible to study each equestrian. The job was becoming laborious. His arms ached from constant use, his legs from inaction. The pipe organ, the bells, the drums beat in his head. He wished he had cotton to plug his ears.

Only three o'clock. He had worked six and a half hours. An hour and half more for a normal day's work!

The children continued to come—would they never have enough? The glitter from the mirrors, brass, and chromium seemed to shine inside his eyes.

Quick, the brass ring. . . Thank goodness he wasn't too late. The gong clanged, the spinning, galloping horses slowed their pace. . . The basket!

Brett hooked the basket on the metal arm and breathed a sigh of relief as he heard the clatter of the returning rings.

"Hey, you, Buckshot," called Jake. "Come down here."

Brett returned the basket to its place and descended the ladder stiffly, full of apprehension. He hadn't made any real mistakes, only near ones.

"You've done enough for one day, kid. My man's come who'll take over."

"Yes, sir," said Brett, glad to be released but not wishing to be fired. Looking at Jake he couldn't be sure which it was. "I—I guess maybe I could do better another time."

Jake's habitual scowl deepened. "You mean you want to come back next week?"

"Sure I do, if you'll hire me."

"Kid, you have me puzzled. Today you done good.

I'm payin' you for eight hours including lunch time."
As he talked he had taken a large roll of bills from his
trouser pocket and peeled off four ones, hesitated, then
handed him a ragged five dollar bill. "Come next Saturday and I'll do the same."

"Oh, thanks. I'll be here. That is if my father lets
me."

"So you did this on your own? I thought as much.
You'll never be back."

"I think I will," Brett said. "If I don't have to go
to our new home."

He exchanged the sweater for his jacket and windbreaker and waved good-by to the old man as well as
Jake. He strode to the subway station on winged feet,
but even before the train pulled out, he fell asleep and
did not awaken until the conductor shook him at the
end of the line. It was nearly seven when he finally
stumbled up the stairs to the studio.

The Accident

THE first thing Brett did on returning home was to slip the tobacco tin under his mattress. He now had $25 for Jerry plus sixty-five cents toward the present. Five more Saturdays at Coney Island and he would have enough—more than enough—for the Acme.

When he had changed into dungarees, he made an itemized accounting of his father's money, as he was supposed to do, taking out the expense of the two Coney Island meals and the chocolate eclair he had just bought. To his relief it came out exactly right, so he put the four dollars and five cents together with the notation on his father's chest of drawers, and went into the kitchen.

Now for a good meal! His father's men friends often bragged about the strange dishes they made up. Brett decided it would be a good time for him to try his hand. As he considered the matter, he made and gnawed on a thick Spam and cheese sandwich.

For one thing, he'd have his old favorite, two shredded wheat biscuits covered with molasses, generously decorated with butter and baked in the oven.

When he had slammed the stove door on this delicacy, he inspected the closet. There wasn't much choice. He emptied a can of tuna fish onto a tin plate and poured over it a can of pork and beans. On top of this he laid slabs of sliced cheese and topped it with strips of bacon. It ought to be good; plenty of it, too. Enough for Sunday's dinner.

He slipped the tin under the broiler, lighted the stove and went into the studio well pleased with himself. This would be a good time to finish his weekly letter to his mother. He pulled out the airmail paper and stared at the wall. He never felt comfortable writing to her for his father had stressed the importance of mentioning nothing that might worry her. Today there was so much he could not tell her, such as how nasty Mrs. Clayton had been, thinking they had bugs, or about his staying home alone this week end. He couldn't even mention his plan to buy Jerry, because he always had his father O.K. his letters and he didn't want his father to know—yet.

So he started by explaining that he had no particular news. The weather had been nice and warm. He got 89 in the math test and maybe he'd have second honors for the month.

Brett was addressing the envelope when he heard a noise like wind in a forest. He got up and turning, saw smoke billowing from the kitchen. As he plunged into the acrid smoke, he saw a yellow tongue of fire licking the stove above the broiler door. Using the oriental rug by the doorway he tried to smother the flames, but it burned through and scorched his hand so that he had to drop it.

Not until then did he think of turning off the gas, but even after that, the roar continued and the smoke grew denser. He considered telephoning the fire department, but he felt he shouldn't leave the kitchen. So far the flames were contained in the stove. The fiery

tongue had ceased to lick the crack of the door and the noise gradually lessened until it ceased. Widening his gaze, he saw smoke spiraling from the rug where a glowing ring still burned. This he easily stamped out, his heel leaving a big hole.

What had started the fire?

Taking a potholder, he cautiously opened the broiler door and saw that his concoction had burned to a crisp.

He opened the window and only then, with the realization that all danger was over, did he feel a fiery pain in his left hand. It was the color and consistency of an overripe tomato.

Moaning aloud he paced the studio, resting the palm of his left hand on the right, his shoulders hunched, his whole body contracted with agony. For the first time in his life, he wished Mrs. McCray were home. He had never burned himself before. Once when his father had, he'd spread on something from a tube. Brett looked in the medicine closet. There were a lot of tubes, but he didn't know which he should use.

A kid in school said his mother put butter on his burn. Brett went to the kitchen and found that the butter had melted in the heat of the fire and most of it had trickled down the leg of the table. Mopping what he could with a paper towel, he tried to apply it, but it did no good.

Long ago, when he had cut his thumb, he remembered, his mother had made him hold it in a pan of salty water. The thought of cold water was pleasing. It might lessen this awful heat. He filled a dishpan, dumped in a stream of salt and submerged his hand. For an instant the shock did seem to check the pain, but then it started up worse than ever, so bad that he couldn't endure it standing still; again he tramped the studio.

He told himself that neither his mother nor Mrs. McCray nor anyone else, for that matter, could do anything. When you were burned, you were burned and no one could unburn you.

He stumbled over the Bocara rug he had tossed to one side. Above the pain, in a sort of upper layer of his brain, he realized what an awful thing he had done. That rug was his mother's dearest possession, the most precious thing she owned, and he had ruined it!

Although he knew all this, he didn't really care, not now he didn't. Later on he supposed he would be very, very sorry, but now he could think of no one but himself.

The old grandfather's clock struck the hour, but it was always fast. Not yet eight and ahead of him stretched the whole night. Hours and hours and hours!

Tears suddenly streamed down his cheeks, and he blubbered like a baby; but this in no way lessened the pain, which finally blanked out all thought until he was conscious only of the agony and the slowness of the passing hours.

The clock chimed nine and he was still walking the floor when he heard feet pounding up the stairs.

"Brett," called his father.

"Dad! You're back ahead of time!"

He had the door open before his father's key reached the lock.

"Yes, B. B. What's happened? You all right? No bad news from your mother?"

"No, Dad. Why didn't you stay until tomorrow?"

"We decided to cut the cost." Mr. Barnes, setting down his suitcase, leaned against the door jamb and closed his eyes. When he spoke, his voice sounded weak. "When did you get back?"

"I didn't go. George's mother didn't want me on account of I ride with Mr. De Luca." Brett had forgotten his determination never to tell his father. "The big dope thought I'd bring bugs." A noisy sob broke from his throat.

"It isn't all that important," his father said, straightening. For the first time he looked at his son. "B. B., what's the matter?"

"I burned my hand, Dad. Maybe it doesn't amount to much, but it hurts fierce."

"Let me see." He held Brett's hand on his own large palm. "Golly, I'll say you did. How? Where?"

"Here. The bacon caught fire."

Mr. Barnes gently returned the injured hand and went to the telephone. "We'll soon take care of that," he said confidently spinning the dial. Then he spoke into the telephone. "Is the Doctor there?"

Modeling

"Gee, Dad, after ten?" Brett jumped out of bed. "I'll never make Sunday School." Then he was stopped short by the pain in his hand, and with it came the memory of the previous night.

They had gone around the corner to Doctor Clay's who said it was a second degree burn, although Brett, for the life of him, didn't see how a first class burn could hurt any more. The Doctor must have agreed with him, for he gave him a tablet immediately to deaden the pain.

The Doctor had cleaned the burn, sprayed it with something, and put on what he called a pressure bandage, which made the hand look like a huge snowball. He sent them home with a sleeping pill, but Brett had not stayed awake long enough to take it.

"Good morning, sleepyhead," his father said coming into his cubicle. "I'm keeping a stack of pancakes hot. Here, put your right arm through the sleeve." He held Brett's bathrobe. "We had to cut off your shirt, remember?"

Brett saw he was in his undershirt and pajama trousers. "How'll I get to school tomorrow?"

"You won't, but Dr. Clay'll put on a smaller bandage tomorrow night. Then you'll be all right." He draped the shabby bathrobe over Brett's left shoulder and tied the sash. "A quiet day won't do you any harm. Think you can wash yourself?"

"Sure, Dad, thanks." Brett felt sorry for his father, always nursing somebody. He felt guilty, too. "I wish I wasn't such a pest, Dad."

"I wish you'd told me you weren't going to George's."

"I was afraid you'd give up your trip."

"How we love to deceive ourselves," Mr. Barnes said cheerfully. "Like cheating at solitaire. Wasn't your real reason a wish to be on your own?"

"Yes, Dad," Brett admitted.

"Well, you've dealt out your own punishment. So we'll consider the misdemeanor bought and paid for, but I hope in the future you'll take your old pa into your confidence." He gave Brett a forgiving slap on the shoulder. "Now hurry. I'm starved."

As Brett washed, his sense of guilt deepened. There was Jerry. Probably his father would think he ought to have been told about the purchase, but somehow, he just couldn't. Maybe because his father didn't like horses.

All through breakfast his conscience bothered him until he told his father about his job at the merry-go-round, and that made him feel better.

"The man said I could work for him every week, but I don't suppose I can for a while."

"Probably not," agreed his father. "Anyway, as soon as we get the deed to the house in Yonkers, we'll spend our week ends out there redecorating."

"It was a good way to make money," sighed Brett.

"Don't worry about that. I spoke to McCray about your modeling for him, and he might use you tomorrow. And there'll be other jobs."

Mr. Barnes got up and, starting for the kitchen, stumbled over the rumpled Bocara rug. He picked it up and looked at Brett through the hole. "B. B., what's this?"

"Oh, Dad, I forgot to tell you. Honestly I did. I used it to smother the flame, but it burned right through onto me."

"So that was it. " Mr. Barnes clenched his jaw. When he spoke, his voice was tight. "B. B., I can't let myself think what might have happened. Don't mention it in your letters to your mother."

"I won't, Dad. Especially about the rug. Don't you suppose it could be mended?"

"Looks plenty ruined, to me."

"Couldn't it be woven, Dad? The tailor around the corner has an ad in his window about weaving."

"It would cost a fortune."

"Mom liked it a lot. She'll miss it when she gets home."

"She might at that. Take it around and see what he'll charge. Hold on—we have fire insurance. I got a letter the other day." Mr. Barnes went to the desk and found the envelope. "Here we are." His confidence gave way to disgust. "It's a notice that the policy has lapsed. Brett, your mother's a better businessman than her husband."

Brett silently agreed. "How much would you spend, Dad?"

"Truth is, Brett, if that commission doesn't come through, we'll need every cent. However, I'd go as high as five dollars."

"Gee, Dad, five bucks! I guess they'd weave anything for that!"

One good thing resulted from the bad week end. That evening when he turned over the change from the five dollars, his father said, "I consider that money the wages of sin. You are the sinner, so it's all yours."

"Gee, Dad, thanks." Brett thought of the burned rug, but he didn't bring up the subject. Instead he went into his cubicle and made a notation. He now had money for Jerry and $5.65 toward the beater.

The next morning he watched his father through the window lugging the newspapers from the apartment house next door.

Promptly as always, Jerry came lumbering up the street. Brett pushed up the window, not without difficulty, and looked down at the animal with possessive anxiety.

"Good morning, Mr. De Luca," he called. "See if you can catch." He tossed a twisted bag containing a carrot and four lumps of sugar into a pair of square, grimy hands. "Jerry all right?"

"Certainly. Why-a not?"

"Close the window, B. B., and let me finish this business," his father called impatiently.

Suppose Mr. De Luca told his father about his plan to buy Jerry! That would spoil everything! Brett knocked on the glass and again worked open the window.

"Dad, you'd better hurry. It's getting late. Mr. De Luca can pay me next Monday."

His father waved him aside, but Brett stood immovable while Mr. De Luca dangled each bundle on a hand scale.

It was evident, when his father returned to the studio, that he had heard no astonishing news.

"Here's forty-nine cents, B. B. I feel as if I'd been shortchanged at least ten dollars, all the hauling."

"Thanks, Dad. Thanks a lot. That's about what I always get." Relief made him garrulous. "He's awful honest, Mr. De Luca is. I'm lucky to have that little business. Maybe in the country I can do gardening."

"Have to get off," his father said, tightening his tie. "I'll be back around six with a good dinner under my arm and after we've eaten we'll go to the Doctor's. Cheer up, tomorrow you'll be back at school."

"I wouldn't mind staying home today so much if you hadn't told Mrs. McCray." Brett dropped the coins he had just received into his bathrobe pocket one by one.

"She'd have found out anyway. Remember, B. B.,

it's kind of her to invite you down there for lunch. Act grateful. Where's your letter to your mother?"

Brett handed him the envelope.

" 'Bye, son, sorry I have to leave you." And Mr. Barnes was off.

Brett didn't object to his father's departure nearly as much as he dreaded Mrs. McCray's arrival.

It was after eleven, however, before she put in an appearance. She wore a starched smock and well-pressed dungarees.

"You poor, poor child," she said, her spectacles magnifying the tears in her eyes. "If anything had happened to you, I *never* would have forgiven myself. Leaving a motherless boy—"

"I'm not motherless," interrupted Brett.

"No, of course not. That was just a way of speaking. I've been so upset since I heard, I haven't been able to sleep. Is the pain very excruciating?"

"Not now it isn't. I'm going to school tomorrow."

"Maybe you will and maybe you won't. You had a very serious burn."

"Only second degree," Brett said.

"Which is much worse than first degree."

"It is?" He felt quite important.

Mrs. McCray sank to the edge of a straight chair. "We're not going to talk about it, are we? Your father tells me you're anxious to model for fifty cents an hour."

He nodded. "Could Mr. McCray use me today?"

"Not him." Mrs. McCray clamped her mouth. "But *I* can use you."

"That's all right, too." Brett tried to sound enthusiastic. Why should he care whether he posed for a sculptor of note or only his amateur-painter wife?

"The idea came to me last night when I couldn't sleep," Mrs. McCray said enthusiastically. "My son, Bill, just returned from a business trip to Hawaii. He brought me some costumes. You could be sitting down, so it wouldn't exhaust you. As I see it, there's the wide ocean to the left, with a departing airplane in the distance. To the right you are sitting under a palm tree, your head bowed in grief. A sort of Madame Butterfly theme. Could be very poignant."

"Sure thing," agreed Brett, neither knowing nor caring what she meant. "And if I had to have my head down, maybe I could be reading."

"Maybe," she said dubiously. "I'll bring up our picnic lunch and afterward paint here."

"That's a swell idea," Brett said with genuine eagerness, for he found the McCray studio very gloomy.

During the lunch of chicken sandwiches, nut cookies, a thermos of hot cocoa and whipped cream—for Mrs. McCray was a good provider—Brett cheerfully answered the many questions regarding the accident. He even showed her the rug and wished he hadn't when she shook her head and clicked her tongue.

"Nothing can be done with that, and your poor mother loved it dearly."

"I know," interrupted Brett. "Maybe it can be woven."

It took Mrs. McCray several trips to carry up her water colors, easel, drawing pad, and costume, for she refused to let Brett do anything.

"All right, you poor boy, I'm ready. Let me help you into the costume."

Brett looked up from his book and stared at a grass skirt, a lei, and a bunch of artificial hibiscus.

"Am I supposed to wear *those*?"

"My dear boy, why not? Very simple. I'll roll up your pajama legs, tie the skirt around your waist, and the flowers around your head."

"But—but, Mrs. McCray, they're for a GIRL!"

She smiled patiently. "What of that? Wearing them doesn't *make* you a girl."

Brett pressed his book to his heart and shook his head. He might have known there would be some gimmick. He needed money, but he didn't need it that much.

"I couldn't, Mrs. McCray. Honest, I couldn't. Wait'll Gladys comes."

"Brett, you wouldn't disappoint me after all my lugging? No one will ever know. Please, dear boy, *please*."

Once he was seated on the modeling stand, his head over a book, his back against a clothes tree (instead of a palm tree), he gradually forgot about the daub of rouge on each cheek, the red flowers over his ears, the grass skirt, and his bare feet. He found this an easy way to earn money.

By three o'clock he had read forty pages and

earned a dollar. After a brief limbering-up period, he returned to the coat tree, this time sitting on a small pillow. Another hour or more had passed when they were interrupted by Mr. McCray, who shouted up the stairs that his wife was wanted.

In no time at all, she was back knocking on the door. Brett rose stiffly to let her in, but instead of Mrs. McCray, her granddaughter Gladys came into the room. At the sight of Brett she gave a silly giggle.

"Gran said you looked pretty as a picture, and she's right. You ought to be a girl."

Brett, in a hot fury, tore off the hibiscus which was no redder than his face and untied the grass skirt, letting it fall to the ground. Making a dive for his cubicle, he grabbed his bathrobe on the way. Never, in all his life, had he been so embarrassed.

Looked like a girl did he? He'd show her. Plunging his right arm into the flannel sleeve, he clutched the robe about him and stepped out scowling fiercely.

"What did you come for anyway?" he asked in his ugliest tone.

"To get my grandmother's things, that's what. If you're going to be nasty, I can be nastier."

"Bet you can't."

"Bet I can. What if I told a girl friend whose brother's in your class about you? That I saw you going around in a girl's skirt with a flower in your hair and rouge on your cheeks!"

This, Brett realized, was no idle threat. If such a story got around the school, he didn't see how he could face the boys. But what could he do to stop her?

While she slammed the tubes of paint into a black tin box, he spit on a handkerchief to wipe off his cheeks and tried to think. He had an idea.

His face relaxed, his lips parted in a smile showing his chipped front tooth of which he was very proud.

"Will you promise, Gladys, not to tell if I give you something you'd like very, very much?" He tried to make his voice soft and corny.

"Of course," Gladys said with delight. "What will you give me?"

"That does it!" exclaimed Brett stalking toward her. "That's blackmail, punishable by law." He glared down at her as she knelt before the box. "If you dare say one word I'll go directly to your grandfather and tell him exactly the kind of girl you are."

"Ugh, you," she snarled. Getting to her feet, she snatched the grass skirt with one hand and the tin box with the other. At the open door she paused. "I always told Gran you were horrid, perfectly horrid."

"Yes," agreed Brett with satisfaction, "I'm a horrid boy and don't you forget it."

Refiguring

WHEN Brett arrived at school the next day, he was welcomed like a hero. The boys mobbed him in the coat room and gazed in awe at his bandaged hand. He learned he had extinguished a great blaze at the risk of his own life, thereby saving his father's valuable pictures and the priceless statues of Mr. McCray.

"Gosh, it wasn't so much," he said modestly.

But the boys would not be cheated of their excitement. Finally the gong sent them to their various classrooms.

That afternoon Mr. De Luca did not lumber into sight until after the last car had departed.

"I was afraid something had happened to you, Mr. De Luca," Brett said as he fed Jerry.

"About yourself you should worry, not me. I did-a not burn myself to charcoal. How is the hand?"

"Fine. I can move my fingers, see? And I'm sure I can drive with one hand, if you'll let me. Is it all right?"

Mr. De Luca communed with himself and finally nodded, inching over on the seat as he did so.

When Jerry had been induced to move, Brett told

Mr. De Luca about the money he made modeling.

"But when I sell-a the horse, I sell-a the wagon," Mr. De Luca said.

With a horse and wagon Brett told himself he could do the marketing; he might even have a little delivery business. "How—how much for the wagon, Mr. De Luca?"

"Fifteen-a dollars."

"That sounds fair," Brett said, but he felt a little worried when he added the two sums. Twenty-five and fifteen equaled forty dollars. A lot of money. "I want them both, please." Brett lost himself in a new dream. He, the owner of a wagon as well as a horse!

"GET GOING!" bawled Mr. De Luca, and Brett realized they had come to a standstill.

Jerry ambled on, and Brett thought about his wagon. He could paint it! A bright blue, or maybe green. He wondered if he could get his father to make a design along the side.

Jerry, without benefit of a driver, clumped around a peanut vendor, but as he dutifully turned in toward the curb the tail of the wagon caught the handle of the peanut cart and tipped it over with a thud of wood and a clatter of bells.

"Whatta you tink yo' doin'?" roared the peanut merchant, waving his arms in a swimming motion over the sea of peanuts.

"Yes, that's a fine way-a to drive, that is!" Mr. De Luca scolded.

"I'm awfully sorry, but I don't think anything's

broken." Brett jumped to the ground and with one hand helped haul the cart onto its wheels. "I'll pick up the peanuts. Every last one." He started in at once, piling them into his hat.

The peanut vendor brought out a pail from under the cart, which facilitated matters greatly. Passers-by paused to watch and advise.

"I'll take a bag," said Mr. De Luca. "The kid'll pay for it when he gets through. That right?" he called.

Brett nodded and went on with his task.

Several other spectators made purchases and while Brett worked, the peanut man called in a soft, coaxing tone, "Peanuts, ladies and gentlemen, nice hot peanuts."

Brett had completed his task when a young policeman in a new uniform came up.

"What yo' think you're doing, boy?"

"He's doin' all right, Officer," the peanut man said cheerfully, and Brett flashed him a grateful smile.

"He's a nice kid."

The young policeman scowled, "All right, all right, but what happened? You can't tie up New York traffic just to play some peanut game."

"It's-a no game. Just a leetle accident. So big," and the peanut man measured an inch with two grimy fingers. "Thez boy, he do not turn quite so far out and topples over my stand. But see, it is all-righted."

The policeman's face brightened. "You say this boy drove the wagon? Come here, sonny."

Brett obeyed.

"What's the matter with your hand?"

"I burned it."

"And you drove with one hand? You have a license?"

"I have a license." Mr. De Luca looked terrified, and his hand trembled as he withdrew a tattered bill-fold from his back pocket.

"You have a license, naturally. But I was told this child was driving. Is that true?"

Mr. De Luca hunched his shoulders and said nothing.

"Well, is it, or isn't it?"

Mr. De Luca raised prayerful eyes. "I didn't mean no harm. I sat beside him. But I never will again, Officer. I promise you. Never."

"Well—I," said the policeman, "all right this time. But we can't have traffic jams in New York City just because children like to drive."

Once more they were on their way. Mr. De Luca held the reins in silence: Brett sat, arms crossed, star-ing ahead of him into a future with but one bright spot that might be extinguished at any moment.

"Will you be wanting me to ride with you any more, Mr. De Luca?"

"I will *not*. Nearly went to jail on account of you."

Brett hesitated, afraid to voice his question, but realizing he must know the truth.

"But you'll still sell me Jerry, Mr. De Luca?"

Mr. De Luca paused while Brett felt his heart beating in his throat. Finally he nodded. "If Papa will let you have him."

"Oh, he will. He wants me to have lots of animals." Brett felt somewhat uplifted. "And you'll buy my old newspapers just the same?"

Again the junk man nodded.

Brett breathed a sigh of relief. He would, at least, see Jerry every Monday. "Then it's settled. When you're ready to sell, I'll buy both Jerry and the wagon."

Standing on the sidewalk he waved his brief case, then hurried home and picked up the oriental rug. The tailor shop was beyond Harrison's and he nodded and smiled at Pegasus. A girl in a bright smock examined the hole, then shook her head.

"No, sonny, we can't do anything like that. You'll have to take it to an oriental rug place." She felt in her hair for her pencil, found it on her ear, and wrote out an address for him.

Brett hurriedly covered the five blocks, for it was getting late. This time he was waited on by a swarthy Armenian who murmured, "Ah, yes, a Bokhara." But at sight of the hole he shook his head. "No, I am sorry."

"You mean it can't be woven?" Brett hadn't anticipated such a possibility, and his heart sank.

"Certainly it *can* be. I could do it myself. I have made rugs. But it is such a big hole and such a small rug it would not be practical."

"It would cost more than five dollars?"

"Many times, perhaps seven."

"Seven dollars?" Brett repeated, feeling vastly relieved.

"Seven times five," corrected the Armenian. "But I have a saddle back rug this size, not new but in perfect condition, that I will sell you for thirty dollars."

The rug he displayed was a silky red with a design of black and glittering white.

"It's a pretty rug," Brett said unhappily, "but even if it were exactly the same it wouldn't do. I wouldn't want to trick my mother. She doesn't know yet."

"And she feels sentimental about it?"

Brett nodded. "It was a wedding present."

"A wedding present, ah, yes, I see." The man's brown eyes gazed into space. "Since it is to save a wedding present, I would weave it for twenty dollars. However, I do not recommend such impractical sentimentality."

Brett's face brightened. "I'm saving now for some special things. When I get enough for them, I'll start saving for the rug. I don't need it until August. How long would it take you?"

"One, two weeks."

"Good. That gives me lots of time." Brett thanked the man and, tucking the rug under his arm, strode home much encouraged.

His father had not yet returned, so he sat down at his own desk and began figuring his expenses. He needed $27.50 for the present, fifteen dollars for the wagon, twenty-five for Jerry, a total of $67.50 before he even considered the rug. Maybe the Armenian was right. He'd forget about it until he had paid for the more important things.

Later his father let out a shrill whistle when told the cost of the repair.

"Nothing doing, B. B. It isn't imperative. Your mother will be so delighted to be home, she'll never give the old rug another thought."

"If I could get a job posing, Dad, I could pay for it."

"You'd be silly, B. B. I'll even have to take back my offer of five dollars."

The telephone rang, and Brett answered it.

"For you, Dad. It's Gus Dockety."

His father greeted his friend, and after a couple of minutes called, "Here's your chance, B. B.; Gus is illustrating children's clothes for a catalogue. He says he could use you evenings from seven to nine for about a week." Mr. Barnes spoke into the telephone. "Could he be studying while he's modeling, Gus? . . . Good." He turned again to Brett. "Want the job?"

"Do I want it, Dad!"

V*isiting*

THE modeling job with Gus Dockety proved dull but profitable. Brett sat on the arm of a chair, on a bicycle, or a table, which became a stone wall. He couldn't study or read as he had with Mrs. McCray, because he had to keep his head up, his eyes in one position; but maybe the inaction helped to heal his burn, for the doctor was amazed at the improvement.

Also, the money he earned cushioned his disappointment when he learned that his allowance would not be increased. The Velskin commission had been given to another artist.

"I was crazy to ever dream of getting it," Warner Barnes said cheerfully. "But we won't starve. I have a small job for Blue-White Starch, and do you know Timmy Hopkins?"

"The little kid in the first form with yellow curls?" Brett was scornful of his own blond hair and any other boy's.

"That's the one," his father agreed. "I'm to paint his portrait for his father's birthday. It'll be a cinch, such a beautiful youngster."

"A sissy, Dad, if you ask me; but I'm glad you got that commission."

The night when Brett came home from Gus's with his job completed, he had to face up with a new disappointment, one that worried him far more than the lost commission.

"We're not getting that house in Yonkers, B. B. I phoned the agent and they can't clear the title." His father sounded mad rather than sad.

"Even so, couldn't we take a chance, Dad?" Brett remembered what awful places they had looked at.

"No. Absolutely NO," his father shouted.

"That means, Dad, we're back where we were when we started looking?"

"Not exactly," his father said, in a calmer tone, looking at his drawing board as if he couldn't waste a minute. "We've combed Connecticut and Westchester, so we can rule them out."

"What if we don't find anything, Dad?"

"We've got to, B. B. I promised your mother we'd have a house in the country by the time she returned, and, by jove, we will!"

"A house, Dad, but maybe not a barn?"

His father shrugged as if a barn were of no particular importance. "There aren't many places with barns. We'll be lucky if we get a garage, but don't worry. On Saturday we'll try our luck in New Jersey."

It was easy to say, "Don't worry," but Brett couldn't help worrying when he knew that he almost owned a horse and had nowhere to put him. He remembered his mother saying once, "It's good, sometimes, to start a thing, even if you can't figure out every detail. The way opens up as you go along." That meant if he could actually buy Jerry, they'd find a barn. So he got himself another modeling job.

Saturday, bright and early, he and his father headed for Jersey, rattling along as fast as their old car could go. They covered seven towns without success.

"Couldn't we take in one more?" Brett asked as his father headed for home. "It's still light."

"Too late for the agents—and for me, also. Fortunately we have plenty of time."

Brett thought of Mr. De Luca's friend. Suppose he quit tomorrow, or even today, where could Jerry be kept?

"I don't think we have a minute to waste, Dad. Mom's been gone five months and we have *nothing*."

"You mean we ought to start out again tomorrow?" his father asked with a groan.

"Yes, I certainly do, Dad," Brett said as if their relationship were reversed. "I can't go. I have Sunday School and a job, but you can. And, Dad, don't settle on a house without even a garage."

Brett walked all the way home from his Sunday modeling job, a matter of forty blocks, partly to exercise his stiff muscles and partly to save the money. He'd have enough on Monday, including his allowance and the paper money, to pay for both Jerry and the wagon.

Now if only his father had found a house with at

least a garage to keep Jerry, he wouldn't worry about a thing in the world, not even the Acme. He could easily earn $28.50.

He was home nearly an hour before his father stamped up the stairs and closed the door with a bang.

"B. B., if you cared anything for your poor father, you wouldn't let him kill himself with Sunday monoxide gas."

Brett knew it had been another wasted day.

The next morning, before going down to collect the newspapers from the apartment house cellar, he slipped his bank into his breast pocket. Ready and waiting at the curb, he sat on the pile of papers and strained his ears to catch the first sound of cowbells.

Eight o'clock, at last, and no sign of Mr. De Luca! A sense of doom possessed him. Jerry—dead. Dead, or maybe dying.

Then he heard the welcome bells and at the sight of the horse and cart—his horse and cart—he jumped to his feet.

"Mr. De Luca, you're late!" he scolded.

"Me, late? No." The junk man reached under the seat and brought up an alarm clock, with hands pointing exactly to eight.

"My watch says two after," Brett said apologetically.

"You should check your time." Mr. De Luca set the whip into the socket and slipped the reins around it, then climbed down while Brett smoothed Jerry's forehead and patted his neck, postponing the pleasant job of feeding him.

Imagine a boy his age buying a living, breathing horse!

Brett swept Jerry's forelock out of his eyes and patted the dusty neck, his fingers making a pattern. "You're all right, old feller. How about a second breakfast?"

While Mr. De Luca tied the stack of papers into bundles with rough rope which he used over and over, Brett fed Jerry leisurely, a lump at a time.

"There you are, sir," he said with a final pat.

"Come-a you here," ordered Mr. De Luca as he hooked one of the bundles on the squeaky scales and held it suspended.

"Nine and a half pounds," said Brett.

"Right," said Mr. De Luca.

They followed the same procedure for each bun-

dle, adding as they went along.

"And now what I owe you?" demanded Mr. De Luca.

"Forty-seven cents."

"Right."

Together they loaded the bundles onto the cart; and while Mr. De Luca dug into his incredibly loose trousers, Brett made the suggestion that had kept him awake most of the night.

"Mr. De Luca, I'd like to buy Jerry and the cart now, today."

Mr. De Luca scowled at him.

"Why you say that? Didn't I tell you I cannot get the auto for one month, maybe two?"

"Yes, I know, but I'd like to *own* Jerry."

"You should ought to be ashamed of yourself to make-a me such a offer."

Brett looked at him in amazement. "Why? You can use him just the same."

"Me, I teach you business." The junk man sounded as if he could cry. "I make you add the weight, watch the scales, count the change. I try to make-a you smart, and you act now like a stupid fool."

"But people pay money down on things. I've heard that all my life."

"A binder, that is different. Two dollars as a binder, that is business, but pay all and get-a nothing, that is foolish folly."

"Then I'll pay a binder," Brett said regretfully. He would much rather feel he was Jerry's owner. He took two dollars from his bank. "Here you are, Mr. De Luca. Now no matter what happens, when you're ready to sell Jerry I can have him and the wagon for thirty-eight dollars?"

Mr. De Luca paused for a moment. He folded the money and tucked it into the depths of his trouser pocket, then nodded. "If-a you change your mind, I will give you back the money. That, too, is not good business. But you are a friend."

He would not leave until he had scratched on a scrap of brown paper:

$40.00
  2.00 paid
$38.00

This he signed with his name.

"Take-a care and keep it. Never lose a receipt."

Brett slipped the paper into his bank. Now that he practically owned Jerry, a stable for him must be found. He had heard his mother say more than once, "Half of getting is wanting." Well, he certainly wanted a stable.

But all the next Saturday they again combed Jersey without finding anything to encourage them.

Brett felt more desperate than ever when on Monday morning Mr. De Luca had some definite news.

"It's goin-a be soon," he said, tapping the scales for Brett's attention.

"What's going to be, Mr. De Luca?" Brett asked, suspecting the truth.

"Alfredo, he's-a worse."

"But he's been worse before."

"Not so worse as this," Mr. De Luca said with satisfaction. "If he quit, or no quit, he will-a sell me his auto in two weeks."

"Oh, two weeks!" Brett breathed a sigh of relief.

"You still want-a my horse and wagon? If no, there is a man—"

"Of course I want it. I paid a binder. You can't sell Jerry to anyone else." Brett grew increasingly excited as he talked.

"I-a know. But where you keep him?"

"We're going to buy a house somewhere in Jersey. Maybe this Saturday. And if there isn't a stable, at least there'll be a garage. Is he in a big stable now, Mr. De Luca?"

"Big enough." Mr. De Luca scowled at the hand full of change he had dug from his pocket. "And when you tell your papa about this horse?" He jabbed an impolite thumb toward Jerry.

"I—I told him I wanted to have horses, and he said I could. We're moving to the country not only for my mother but so I can have animals."

"But when you tell Papa?" he insisted.

This was a question Brett did not like to face. "When I actually own Jerry, that's when."

Mr. De Luca handed him five dimes and a penny

"What-a I say now is not-a good business, but I think your papa say, 'No, you cannot have the horse.' If-a so, I give you back your two dollars. That is bad business, but it is fair."

"Sure, it's fair, Mr. De Luca. You're always fair."

As Brett walked to school, he recalled his father's theory that worry never helped anything. He suspected that Jerry slept in a little shed. Certainly such a place shouldn't be hard to find. So, as he pushed aside his apprehensions and strode to school, he held his head high, proud of his possession.

George passed him in his car and got out to walk with him.

"It's definite about Jerry. I'll own him in two weeks."

"Found a house yet?"

"No, but we will."

"I just wish you hadn't crossed off Westchester. Hold on a sec, I have something for you." Holding his brief case on a raised knee, he opened it and extracted a square envelope addressed to Brett. "Here, take it. It won't bite."

Brett withdrew a folded sheet and tried to read the hurried script; but he made such a bad job of it that George snatched the note out of his hand and read: "Dear Brett, I cannot tell you how sorry I am about George's invitation a few weeks ago. I had so much on my mind at the time, I didn't seem to realize *you* were the boy who drove the junk cart. Of course George shouldn't have told you my silly reason, but since he did, please excuse me and prove that you have forgiven me by spending this week end with us. Sincerely, Retta Clayton."

"Well?" George asked reclaiming his brief case. "What do you say?"

"Golly, George! Golly! Everything nice seems to be happening to me!"

"You'll come?"

"You bet I'll come. Sure thing. Now that everything's practically settled about Jerry, I've got to hurry and learn to ride horseback."

George wrinkled his nose. "Look, B. B., do you really think you can make a saddle horse out of Jerry?"

"Why not?" demanded Brett. "If I put a saddle on him, why isn't he a saddle horse? I don't expect him to jump fences and stuff like that, but I bet it will be easier for him to carry me than it is to pull the wagon."

"Maybe," George said, but he didn't sound convinced.

This second invitation to Ridgeview did not stir up the excitement of the first because Brett had so many things to think about. Mainly, he still had the problem of Jerry to solve. Not that he was worried, but he would certainly feel better when they had found a home.

Friday afternoon Martin, the Claytons' grumpy chauffeur, called for the boys at school. Brett hoped he and George would drive to Ridgeview alone, but no such luck. First they picked up Mrs. Clayton. She made a big fuss over Brett which wiped out all thought of his old hurt, and made him decide that she was really quite nice but not in any way as pretty as his mother. Then he learned that they were stopping for George's sister, Carol.

"Oh." Brett's heart sank, for he considered all girls pests. "Is she older than you?"

"A year younger. Birthday in August, when's yours?"

"August fifteenth."

"About your age. She likes horses."

"Oh." That made it better.

She was not at all like Gladys, he discovered. She was thin and flat and looked straight at him without blinking an eyelash.

"Brett Barnes, I'm glad to finally meet you. George says you're batty about horses."

"Batty?" discouraged her mother.

"Oh, Mom, darling, please, this is such an important subject. George says you're buying a horse out of your own money."

Brett turned around and knelt in his seat, the better to talk to her.

"That's right. George doesn't think much of Jerry, but I love him."

"George is all right except about horses. Mom, darling, I'm starved. Can't we stop at Schraffts?"

A soda at Schraffts was a real treat to Brett. He hadn't bought one since he'd started saving for the Acme.

They had a further delay while Mrs. Clayton did an enormous amount of marketing, but when they finally got started it took them scarcely more than an hour to reach Ridgeview village which consisted of a block of stores, a church, and a movie house.

"Uncle Dave, who owns the riding academy, lives around the corner from the movie," explained George.

"In a precious old house that our great grandfather built and our darling grandfather lived in all the days of his life," added Carol.

"And you might also say it was your mother's birthplace," called Mrs. Clayton from the front seat.

"You must have all felt terrible when you knew about the movie," sympathized Brett.

Carol gave a tooting laugh. "We were all delighted! Gramp sold the property himself for a lot of money. He sold all the property except the house and less than an acre of ground. He was awful smart and I wish he'd lived to be a hundred. Mom, can't we stop in for a second? I'd like Brett to see Aunt Lucy."

"No, dear," Mrs. Clayton said firmly, "but Martin will drive by, if you like."

"Aunt Lucy's such a darling. Isn't she, George?"

"Not bad," conceded her brother.

"They're building a big modern house—"

"That's right," interrupted George. "It'll be finished soon, and then they're going to sell the old house. There's something for you to buy, B. B."

"Do you want a house?" asked Carol.

"Sure he does and there's a stable, too."

"I guess it would be too expensive," Brett said remembering Westchester prices.

"Naw, it's got to go cheap on account of nobody wants to live next to a movie, but honest it isn't bad." George grew increasingly enthusiastic. "Carol's right when she says it's a nice old house, and it would be fun to have you up here."

"That part would be wonderful," agreed Brett not willing to consider such a desirable solution. "But—"

Martin had driven up a side street and now turned again around the movie house.

"It's right after that brick wall—keep your eyes peeled," ordered Carol. "There, starting with that white picket fence. You really don't see much of the house. It's built with the side to the road."

She was right, Brett hadn't seen much and what he saw didn't impress him.

"Even if it's an awfully nice house, I'm afraid my father wouldn't want to be so near the village."

"Of course he wouldn't," called Mrs. Clayton. "Don't nag about it, children; we want Brett to have a good time."

It started to rain the next morning as they were eating breakfast, a sullen, determined rain.

"Will we ride anyway?" Brett asked hopefully.

Carol shook her head. "But maybe it'll clear."

"It won't even be clear tomorrow," predicted George, and he was right. However, he and Carol called up their friends and invited them to the house. Both Saturday and Sunday flew by faster and more pleasantly than Brett would have thought possible.

As he mounted the studio stairs on Sunday night, he told himself it had been a good week end, although he had not even seen a horse. Now, if his father had found a house to buy, he could relax and really be happy.

Revising

"Hi, Dad, I'm home."

"Hello, B. B., glad to see you." His father stood working on the Harkness portrait with the help of a day lamp. "Sorry you had such rotten weather."

"I know, but we enjoyed ourselves just the same." Brett set his suitcase on the floor and sent it sliding toward his cubicle. "Any news about a house?"

His father shook his head. "Not a peep from anyone."

"But, Dad, didn't you look at anything?"

"Oh, yes, B. B., I've done plenty of looking. Most of my waking hours, since you've been away, I've looked at this blooming canvas."

That meant he hadn't gone anywhere, hadn't tried to find a house.

"But don't worry, son," Mr. Barnes said cheerfully, "we still have over three months."

Afraid his annoyance might make him rude, Brett muttered, "I'll go unpack," and disappeared in his cubicle.

He tried to concentrate on his term essay, HORSES

VERSUS AUTOMOBILES, but every time he wrote
the word horse he thought of poor Jerry. In Brett's mind
he seemed to grow older and weaker each second until
he finally slumped between the splintery shafts and,
deaf to Mr. De Luca's "Git-up," breathed his last. There
he lay, stiff and cold in death.

Throwing down his pencil, Brett went back to the
studio ready to talk about anything, rather than sit
alone with his thoughts.

"How about your week end, B. B.? So you had a
good time in spite of the weather?"

"A swell time, Dad. They're swell people. I only
wish we could find a house somewhere near them."

"Me, too, but not a chance." His father wiped his
brush on an old rag. "We did Westchester, remember?"

Brett nodded. "But, Dad, George says his grandfather's house is for sale. An old farm house. George
says there's a stable, too."

Mr. Barnes interrupted the talk to apply a dash
of cobalt to the background. "Doubtless there are lots
of old farmhouses for sale—" He mumbled his words
because he held a brush between his teeth. "But none
we can afford."

"George says this is going cheap. It must be a nice
house, Dad. George's uncle still lives in it. He's the one
that owns the riding academy, a swell joint. He has
dozens and dozens of horses. I guess he makes a wad
of money. They're building a dumb old ranch house.
That's why they're selling. George says it isn't exactly
on the market yet, but it will be *soon* and it's going

very cheap."

"Must be a reason," his father said slowly as he deepened the shadow under the Harkness boy's eye.

"That's right, Dad, there is a reason. It's sort of near the movie house. Bunks up to one side of it at the back, I think. But that might not be so bad."

"Doesn't sound too good," his father said.

"But, Dad, couldn't we just look at it?"

"We could—if we had time and money to throw away. Honestly, B. B., do you think for one moment that your mother would like it?"

"No, Dad," Brett admitted bravely. "But, gosh, I'm getting kind of worried."

"We still have time." But he knew by his father's voice, that he, too, was worried. "We'll try northern Jersey this week. Can you come with me?"

"No, Dad. I'm booked up." He was glad he was, for much as he wanted a house, he hated house hunting even more than his father did.

The next morning as Jerry lifted his sagging lips to gather the carrot into his mouth, Brett gazed at him in pity.

"Your papa buy-a a house yet?" demanded Mr. De Luca.

"N-no, not exactly," Brett answered trying not to worry. "He may settle on something this Saturday, or maybe Sunday. Mr. De Luca, the other man, the one who wants to buy Jerry if—if I can't, what would he use him for?"

"For truckin'."

Brett winced. "Do—do you think Jerry would be strong enough?"

Mr. De Luca shrugged inside his loose coat. "That-a his worry."

"Well, it won't be his worry because *I* want Jerry, and I'll be very kind to him."

It was hard, however, as the days passed, to keep up his courage, for his father, busy on the portrait, seemed to have forgotten that they were practically homeless; he didn't even look at the ads in the paper at night.

Thursday he boasted at dinner, "Well, B. B., your old man isn't such a total loss after all. Today I got three orders, not too big, but not too little either. I'm getting in your class. Guess I'll have to stay home over the week end and work."

"*Dad!* You're not serious?" Brett found it impossible to contain himself.

"I am, as a matter of fact. If I can earn the money, we can find the house."

"But, Dad, remember what that agent said about it being a matter of luck? That sometimes people had to sell, and if you were around and could snap it up, you'd get a fine bargain. Remember?"

"What a slave driver you are, son. Would you let me off Saturday if I promise to go Sunday?"

Brett gave a faint grin. "Just so you don't miss a bargain."

"And speaking of work, B. B., aren't you overdoing this modeling business? Do you have to work like a dog to buy a dog?"

"It isn't so awful boring, Dad. Miss Elsa and Miss Green let me prop up a book so I can read or study."

"Tell them to use a Polaroid camera the way I do," suggested his father.

Brett shook his head. "I will not. It's a good way to earn money."

"Well, I'll be glad to see a little more of you, even if I haven't time to look at you." And Warner Barnes laughed as if he hadn't a worry in the world.

Sunday morning Brett waved his father off and dressed for Sunday School. After a lonely dinner at the Automat he went to Miss Green's and modeled for four hours, broken mid-way by tea and crackers.

All afternoon, for no definite reason, Brett felt that something good was about to happen. When he got home and took one look at his father, he knew by the gleam in his eyes, the arch of his eyebrows, the curve of his mouth, that the hunch was right.

"Find a house, Dad?"

"Better than that, son. Better than anything you can imagine. I just had a telephone call. Guess who? Who'd you most rather hear from than anyone in the whole world?"

Brett's cheeks flushed scarlet. But it couldn't be—hadn't she made the rule herself. "No transatlantic telephoning," she had said. "Too expensive, and also voices can make you more homesick than letters."

"Dad, not—not—?"

"That's right. Your mother." His father's voice

grew husky, and getting up he paced the length of the studio, pausing to look out the blank window while Brett took in the significance of the news.

"But, Dad, why did she telephone when she wouldn't let us?"

"Because she couldn't wait." He kept his back toward Brett. "She's cured. She's flying home the fourteenth of May."

"The fourteenth," whispered Brett.

"Yes, less than three weeks. Two weeks from Thursday."

Brett's tripping heart raced even faster. Would he have time to earn the Acme money?

"And a house for her, Dad? Did you find one?"

"Sit down, B. B." His father pulled up a chair and faced him. "I promised your mother I'd have a house for her when she returned."

"Yes, Dad, I know."

"Here's a bit of luck. We can rent a little furnished house in Oradell, for six months with an option if they decide to sell. The owner's trying out a new job in Detroit. That'll give your mother time to look around herself. Get the idea?"

Brett nodded. "One of those ranch houses?"

"A nice one, B. B. Easy to take care of, a terrace in the back with an outdoor grill; a dishwasher, clothes washer, all that stuff, and soaked in sunlight."

Brett felt sure he knew the answer before he asked. "A barn, Dad?"

His father shook his head. "Not even a garage.

But in six months I'm sure we could find something better."

Six months! What would he do with Jerry?

His father must have seen his disappointment, for he went on, "If you vote against it, B. B., we'll keep on looking; but the agent tells me this'll be snapped up, and I can't bear to have your mother let down."

"No, Dad, of course not." Brett swallowed a lump.

"The owner's given me until the first mail Tuesday. If you agree, I'd get off a binder tonight." His father looked at him questioningly. "Hold on a second, I have a picture. Need it in one of my jobs." He gave Brett a Polaroid print of a house. "Very neat, you see."

"Yes," agreed Brett.

"No animals—no dog. The woman's fussy. But it isn't for always."

"I know, Dad."

"And you'll put up with it?"

"Yes, Dad. Sure. Of course." Brett cleared his throat. "Let me mail your letter, Dad, it's raining."

H*iding*

O<small>N</small> winged excitement Brett covered the distance to the mailbox. His mother would be home in less than three weeks—cured! Not the tired, discouraged invalid she'd been for so long before she went away, but her gay, merry self!

Of course this settled the problem of Jerry. Poor, poor old Jerry. It would mean the trucking business for him. On the other hand, there would be plenty of money for the Acme and the rug.

It was not until that evening after supper, when he settled down to do some more work on his term essay, that he began to realize what giving up Jerry really meant to him. How often, in his imagination, had he curried the shaggy coat until it shone like satin; how many times had he painted the wagon. He knew without a doubt that the man who wanted to buy Jerry would kill him with work. The thought was more than he could bear.

Feeling as he did, he found it impossible to write about horses; so he went to bed, but not to sleep. As the grandfather's clock chimed the quarter hours, his thoughts spun about Jerry: poor old creature dragging heavy loads for the new owner. He'd be dead in no time, and Brett would be responsible. In his happiness about his mother, he'd forgotten his responsibility toward a helpless animal. If he'd objected to that furnished house, his father never would have rented it. They might have found exactly what they wanted next Saturday, or the Saturday after. But now it was too late.

Probably, if his mother were here, she'd arrange to have Jerry boarded until they had a stable.

Why hadn't he thought of that before? He, himself, could pay for Jerry's board until she returned; that is if he postponed buying the Acme. And now that she was well and strong, she didn't really need an electric beater; and anyway, he'd keep on saving and buy the Acme later.

Comforted by the thought that he could have both his mother and his horse, he finally fell asleep.

The next morning as he fed Jerry, he told Mr. De Luca the wonderful news. "She arrives in Idlewild at 4:30 two weeks from next Thursday," he said, his eyes dancing.

"So soon, eh? I tink she not want you to have the horse."

"Oh, you're wrong. She's crazy about horses. That part's all right. My one trouble is we've rented a little house without even a garage, but—"

"Then you no can buy him." Mr. De Luca sounded pleased. "And a good thing, too. He too old, you too young. I give you back your money."

"But I *do* want him, Mr. De Luca. Of course I want him. How much longer will you need him? A month, maybe?"

"Not-a so long. A week, a day, who can tell? Best I return your money."

"No, Mr. De Luca. When you have to sell him, I'm ready to buy him and pay his board. Don't worry, I have the money."

Mr. De Luca shook a stubborn head. "You can no board him where I keep him. If my friend no buy Jerry, he buy some other horse and he need the stall."

"Then I'll find another stable," Brett said, refusing to be discouraged. "There are plenty of stables in the city."

Mr. De Luca shrugged and began weighing the papers. In parting, after he had "git-upped" Jerry into slow motion, he muttered, "Your papa and your mama, they no let you buy Jerry."

Brett, pretending not to hear, called cheerfully, " 'Bye, Mr. De Luca, see you next Monday, and Jerry, don't you worry about anything."

He told George about his mother's unexpected return as he and his class were being driven to Central Park in one of the school buses, for physical exercises. "She'll arrive at Idlewild at 4:30 P.M. exactly eighteen days from today."

"Gosh, that's wonderful!" exclaimed George. "Your father find a house yet?"

"Yes. In Jersey."

"*Jersey?* Why'd you let him?"

"He's only renting for a few months. We had to have something for Mom. I'm not making any fuss, but it doesn't even have a garage."

"Which means you can't buy that bag of bones."

"It means nothing of the kind; and I was looking for help, not insults." Turning away from George, Brett stared out of the window.

"Look, Brett." George dug him with his elbow. "I'm not sorry if you can't buy Jerry, but I am sorry you're sorry. How can I help you? Tell me that."

"I was wondering," said Brett deciding not to stay mad, "if you had any idea what it costs to board a horse in the city."

"Sure, I know exactly. My sister wanted to bring in her horse. Ninety-two dollars and fifty cents in a regular stall and a hundred dollars in a box stall."

"I don't mean by the year," explained Brett.

George gave a disagreeable laugh. "Who said anything about a year? That's a month."

"Jeepers," groaned Brett. "But it wouldn't cost anything like that in the country, would it?"

"It isn't peanuts," said George.

"I mean—it'll be summer and couldn't he be put out to pasture?"

"You sure do want that mangy—that ancient horse," George said, shaking a puzzled head. "Tell you what, I'll be seeing my uncle this week end. He's wacky about horses, too, like my sister. I told him about you and Jerry, and he can understand your devotion. Suppose I ask his advice?"

"Wish you would, George. Trouble is, I haven't much time. Mr. De Luca may have to sell Jerry any minute. You won't forget?"

"I sure won't. Fact is, Brett, I'm beginning to hope you can buy him."

"And tell your uncle I have money to pay for his board, if it isn't too steep."

"I'll tell him, and I bet he works out some plan," said George.

Relieved in mind about Jerry, Brett threw himself into a game of baseball. However, on his way home from school he walked blocks out of his way to check at a livery stable and learned that George had been right.

He reached home ahead of a gathering storm and found his father ready to leave.

"Hi, B. B. I'm due at Peroni's opening, and I'm eating at the Lotos Club. Want to come along?" When Brett shook his head, his father peeled off two dollar bills. "Here. Go to the Automat. No home cooking."

"O. K., Dad."

He echoed his father's cheerful good-by and changed into dungarees and a sweater. He must get his closet cleaned before his mother returned, and there was no time like the present.

The telephone interrupted him as he stood wondering where to begin. It was George, speaking in an excited tone. "Brett, listen. Uncle Dave's at Harrison's. Mom says he just phoned. She didn't know I wanted to speak to him. Hurry around there and you'll meet him."

"How'll I know him?"

"Wait in his car, a station wagon. He never locks it. It's in a tow-away zone, but they let him park in front of the door. Get going."

"Sure, sure. Thanks." Brett went back for his tin bank which he thrust into his hip pocket and pounded down the stairs.

The sky had darkened. Thick clouds gathered in the west and a gusty wind blew at his back as he ran around the block. A station wagon, a very shabby one, stood in front of Harrison's, with one of their paper bags hooked over the handle, for it was in a no-parking zone.

He leaned against the door and listened to the approaching storm. Uncle George would want to get started immediately. Maybe, Brett thought, he'd better ride with him to some nearby station and take the train back. He was thankful he'd brought his bank. A raindrop hit his nose. He tried the door, found it unlocked, and slipped into the rear seat.

The pungent, horsy odor of the plaid blanket beside him was pleasant. Looking behind him he saw an assortment of interesting things piled on top of the spare tire: a new saddle, an old bridle, some stirrups. His inspection was interrupted by an authoritative voice.

"That your car?"

It was a policeman. Before Brett could gather his wits to answer, a deep voice with a southern accent drawled, "That's right, Officer."

The policeman, he realized, spoke, not to him, but

to a lanky man wearing a large, western hat, who yanked Harrison's bag off the handle and opened the door.

Brett, anxious to remain unseen, slid lower in the seat.

"I see by your license plate, you're from Texas," the policeman said with sudden friendliness.

"That's right. Fort Worth, to be exact."

Brett's eyes widened in amazement. He'd *hopped into the wrong car!*

"I was born in El Paso," boasted the officer.

"Thought you was a Texan. You-all sounded that way."

Brett slid lower in his seat, out of the officer's sight.

"Reckon you don't realize you're in a no-parkin' area. Sorry, but you'll have to get goin'."

"Thanks for tellin' me, Officer." The Texan got in and slipped under the wheel. "O.K. to wait for my boss? He'll be along in a second."

"Well—make it snappy." And the policeman continued on his way.

While Brett waited for him to get out of ear's reach, the door slammed and the car started off.

"Glad you beat the rain, Boss. See you got the automatic."

Brett swung around, looked at the back of two heads, and let his jaw hang slack. What should he do?

"Yes," said the boss. "A Cody 42." There was a rustle of paper.

"Sweet baby," said the Texan. "Did you remember

the shells?"

"Naturally."

"Then we're all set—"

"If it's necessary."

"That's right. Don't think I'm lookin' forward to it. I ain't. I said I'd do it if I had to, and I promise you I won't botch the job. When I shoot, I shoot to kill."

Brett suddenly realized his danger. He was always seeing gunmen on TV, but he had never expected to get mixed up with them.

There was only one thing for him to do. Lie low. Sometime they'd have to leave the car—for dinner certainly, if not before. Moving noiselessly, as one can when one's life depends on it, he stretched out on the floor of the car and hid himself under the horse blanket. Indifferent to the stifling heat, he scarcely dared to draw a breath.

The storm broke. Brett heard the rain pounding on the roof; thunder exploded loud as blockbusters. Wind shook the old car, but it rattled on, stopping only for traffic lights.

The road became smoother. They must be on a parkway. Brett made an air tunnel. Carefully he shifted his position, for his tin bank had been digging into his back. And that was another thing. If they caught him, they'd steal all his money—and he had a lot. Counting the two dollars his father had given him and his dollar allowance, he had $58.00. No one would even know about it, and his mother would never get her Acme.

He should have given up the whole idea of buying

Jerry when he realized he had no place to keep him. If
he had stuck to his original plan, he would have bought
the Acme today; and what's more, he'd have enough
money left to fix the rug which lay rolled up and forgotten under his bed.

That's exactly what he should be doing; and in
that case, he wouldn't be here. If he ever escaped, he
vowed his wealth would go for the Acme and the rug—
not Jerry.

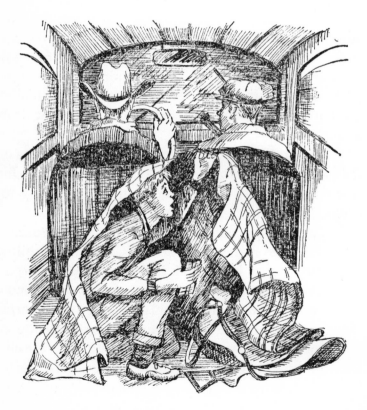

This decision comforted him, somehow. He began to think about his mother and how pleased she'd be with the beater, and how much easier life would be for him if he didn't have to worry about Jerry. Why, it had kept him awake half the night. He yawned.

But he mustn't go to sleep. They'd probably be stopping soon. If they locked him in, he'd climb over the back of his seat, find a wrench, and smash the glass in the rear.

But he must keep awake.

In the midst of a yawn he saw the Boss lean over the back of his seat and stare down at him.

"You, kid, there," he said, "you're not as safe as you think you are. You haven't been fooling me—not for a minute. We're just waiting, Tex and me, until we get to a lonely spot to dump you out." He gave an evil laugh. "We'll let you go on your own feet. A little distance, that is. Tex is surefire." Again he laughed.

Brett hugged his body which vibrated with the pounding of his heart. He was too frightened to think; too frightened to feel anything but fright.

"Get going," ordered the Boss much as Mr. De Luca bawled at Jerry.

Brett made no motion to obey.

"Get going," repeated the Boss, "unless you want to join us. Is that right? Want to be part of our gang? We could use a kid like you. It's the only way you'll get out alive, and a live gunman's better than a dead kid."

"That's a lie!" exclaimed Brett and jumped to his feet.

He knew himself to be a hero. He was sacrificing his life for that which was right, but his courage would go unhonored and unsung.

"If that's your decision, it's your funeral," the Boss said cheerfully. "Here, Tex, here's the gun. Shoot him and shoot to kill."

A deafening shot lifted Brett off the floor and dropped him back again.

An Offering

BRETT awoke from his instantaneous dream. He was so hot he flung the blanket off his face, and so cold he shivered.

"Heck, a blowout," rasped Tex as the car skidded onto a soft shoulder and came to a stop. "Lucky it's not raining."

Brett heard the doors open and slam shut, heard gritty footsteps, the creak of a hinge as the back of the station wagon was opened. Could he make his escape now? He raised himself to peek over the back of his seat, then ducked and pulled up the blanket. Tex was freeing the tire from the assorted luggage.

Later, Brett felt the car mount on the jack, heard them kick off the wheel and kick on the other. Yes, it would be best to do nothing—just stay under cover.

"Hi, Boss, where's the horse blanket?" Tex called, his head in the luggage compartment. "I want to throw it over the muddy wheel."

Brett tucked it more securely about his head and clung to it fiercely.

"I see it," shouted Tex.

Brett lost the tug-of-war. The blanket was wrenched from his grasp, and as he stared up into a pair of startled eyes, he knew this time it was no dream.

"Holy Moses, kid, what are you doing here?" Before Brett could answer the man shouted, "Boss, come see what I uncovered!"

Just as in the dream, another head appeared.

"Tex, where's the gun?"

"Hold on, Boss. Don't scare the kid's pants off him."

"Maybe you don't have juvenile delinquents in Texas. Sit up, boy. Put your hands up."

Brett obeyed.

"What's your story?"

"I'm not talkin', see," Brett snarled in his toughest tone. Let them think he was a sneak thief. Let them suppose he was one of them.

"Gosh, he don't look so tough," Tex said regretfully.

"Frisk him, will you, and I'll find some rope."

Tex climbed over the back of the seat and, making Brett stand up, ran his hand over his body. He paused at the feel of the tin box and took it out.

"A kid like you smoke a pipe?" he asked in a sad tone; but when he pulled out the roll of bills all kindness left his voice and his eyes were hard as marbles. "Guess you're not so far off, Boss. There's real money here."

The Boss handed Tex a length of rope.

"Why did you hide there?" the Boss asked sternly.

"Because I wanted to. That's why. See." And Brett

parted his lips so that his chipped tooth would show.

"Tie him up, Tex. I'll pack the tools."

Tex tied his hands behind him and his ankles together with one piece of rope.

"Kid," he said, as he was leaving, "I'm tellin' you the truth. It don't pay."

Outside Brett heard him ask the Boss, "What'll you do with him?"

"Turn him over, I suppose."

"Then what'll happen?"

"A reformatory, I suppose."

"Poor kid. Couldn't we stop at your house first? I'll bet your wife'd make him talk."

Brett thought he heard the Boss chuckle as he said, "That's dangerous. She'll want to adopt him."

He sounded so kindly, so nice, it was hard to think of him as a gunman; but maybe, in some ways, they were human, too. It was all very bewildering.

Once again they sped along the highway and soon took an exit marked HIGH ST.—in what town? They passed houses where life went on as usual: a little girl called, "Here, Pussy, Pussy, Pussy." It seemed hard to believe that thousands and millions of people were living natural lives.

He wondered if he ought to call out for help, but tha⁺ meant winding down the window; and when he tried to do that, they'd nab him.

As they passed a cluster of ranch houses, Tex turned suddenly in the opposite direction and swung the car onto a driveway of crushed stone. He drew up before a large house built at right angles to the road, and shut off by a high hedge.

A girl in blue slacks and a crimson blouse dashed out of the house, the screen door slapping after her. Her fair hair, wound about her head in braids, reminded Brett of his mother.

"Dave, darling, you're late. What happened?" The girl flung her arms about the Boss's neck as he climbed out of the car.

"Had a flat. How's Twinkletoes?"

"Better. Dr. Miller says she'll be all right."

"Thank God," the Boss said fervently. "I expected I'd have to shoot her tonight."

"He means *I'd* have to shoot her," corrected Tex. "That's sure wonderful news."

"Oh, but you don't know all of it. Her colt died this afternoon."

"Better the colt than the mare," answered Tex.

"Yes, Lucy, she'll have other colts. And we have another problem."

The problem sat pressing his stomach while he adjusted his mind to this latest explanation. So they'd bought a gun to kill a horse—a brood mare. And furthermore, hadn't the Boss called the girl Lucy? And hadn't she called him David? Aunt Lucy and Uncle David. Then he hadn't gotten into the wrong car.

He tried to stifle a laugh that grew uncontrollably higher and higher.

"Who's that, Dave?" Not waiting for an answer, she looked into the car. "Dave, Tex, what's all this?"

She climbed into the back seat and tried to untie the rope. "Why, you two big bullies!"

"Hold on, Lucy, let Tex do that—but see that he doesn't escape. He's a hard-boiled delinquent if ever I saw one."

"I'm not. No, I'm not," Brett said between bursts of laughter that ended in sobs. He kept his gaze on Lucy, while Tex worked with the rope. "It's all—all a mistake. I'm George's friend. We're in school together."

"Of course there's been a mistake," Lucy said soothingly. "I can see by your face you're a wonderful boy. We'll get you in the house, and you can tell us everything. Men can be so stupid!"

Brett shook his head. "I—I was the stupid one."

"There you are, son," Tex said winding the rope over his hand and elbow.

"Now, come on in," Lucy invited hospitably.

"Just a second, Lucy," Dave said. "If you're ready to talk, boy, what's your name?"

"Brett Barnes."

"Brett Barnes!" exclaimed Lucy. "You don't mean you're B. B.? The boy who's buying Jerry!"

Brett nodded.

"Then why didn't you tell me?" Dave demanded, annoyed.

"I—I thought you were a gunman. You had a gun and spoke of killing. So I pretended I was a dead-end kid."

"Oh, the poor darling." Lucy sounded as if she could cry. She sat beside him and slipped her arm through his.

"Ask him, Lucy, why he hid in the car," Dave said through the window.

By now Brett had checked his hysterics and was able to tell them how George had phoned that his Uncle Dave was parked in front of Harrison's. "I felt a drop of rain, so I went in the car. When the cop said something about a Texas license plate, I thought I was in the wrong car; but before I could say anything, the Boss gets in with a gun he'd just bought and they talked about killing somebody—so I thought I was in the hands of gunmen."

Tex nodded his head. "It was my car. We did give you pretty rough treatment. I'll say that for us."

"You were brutes—both of you—tyrants, barbarians, swashbucklers. It's a marvel the poor boy wasn't frightened out of his reason. Come on, B. B., we'll phone your home and tell them why you're late."

"There's only my father, and he won't be back for hours." Brett followed her out of the car as he talked, working his stiff legs with difficulty. "If I can have my money, please, I'll take the next train home."

"Before dinner! Indeed you won't. We're all going to have delicious beef stew and apple pie. That includes you, too, Tex." And the hostess hurried ahead of them into the house.

"I'm sorry for my part in this blood-and-bullet comedy, Brett," Dave said pausing at the door and holding out his hand. "I should have known, by looking at you, you were no dead-end kid."

Brett smiled sheepishly as they shook hands. "That goes for me, too, Sir."

"I'm the villain in the show," Tex said, getting out the tin box. "I swiped the boodle. Here, kid, here's your fortune."

They stepped directly into a big country kitchen with a coal stove on which a busy tea kettle sent out puffs of smoke, and an iron pot filled the air with the odor of simmering beef stew.

"Lucy, your new house won't be as good as this," Tex said lumbering in. "If I had me a wife, I'd buy it myself."

"If you even had a girl, we'd save it for you," Lucy answered, setting two more plates on a round center table. "Show our forgiving guest where he can wash for dinner."

Brett followed Tex down a hall past a number of open doors to a bathroom gay with bright wallpaper and yellow paint.

"This is an awful nice house," he said. "I wish my father had seen it."

"You're darned right, it's a swell place; but Dave says nobody'll buy it on account of the movie house. It wouldn't bother me. No, sir. I'd like to have a movie so handy." Tex gave a hearty laugh and left Brett to wash away the tear stains and grime.

"Well, you're certainly handsome, with your hair slicked and everything," said Lucy when he returned to the kitchen. "Sure your father won't worry?"

"No, not if I can get home by ten."

"Easy," called Dave who had changed into a red plaid shirt and looked like a boy. "There's an eight-ten due in New York at nine-thirty. Can you make it from the station in half an hour?"

"I can walk it in ten minutes," Brett said, drawing a deep, contented breath. My, but he was starved!

"One thing I don't understand," Dave said when they were all served. "Why did you want to see me, B. B.?"

"Oh, that deal's all off, now," Brett mumbled. Then realizing he must give some explanation, he went on, "You see my father has rented a dinky ranch house so he'll have a place to take my mother—"

"Now I have you all sorted out in my mind," interrupted Lucy. "Your father's the Cluett art teacher, and your mother's in England recuperating. Isn't she due home in August?"

"She's cured. She'll be home two weeks from Thursday."

"How wonderful!" breathed Lucy, as if it were her own mother.

"Yes, almost too wonderful." Brett cleared his throat.

"And you started to explain why you wanted to see me," prompted Dave patiently.

"Yes, sir. I wanted to know about a place to board Jerry because this house we're renting hasn't even a garage. George said to ask you—you'd know. But that deal's all off. I've decided *not* to buy Jerry—definitely."

"Maybe that's wise," Dave said, much as George

might have.

"Maybe," agreed Lucy, "and then again, maybe not." She turned to Brett. "I suppose your father's rented a house because he can't find anything to buy." Brett nodded. "He ought to look at this place, B. B. There's a big stable and half an acre of ground."

"Yes, I know," Brett said nodding. "I did tell my father, and he wouldn't consider it. Just the same, I wish he'd looked at it."

"I do, too. I'd love to have an artist living here," Lucy said. "I'm as interested in painting as I am in horses. Speaking of horses, why aren't you buying Jerry? It must be a very recent decision. George told me it was all settled."

Brett said it was and took a drink of water.

"But why?" insisted Lucy.

Brett shrugged. "I—I guess the idea always was foolish."

"Too expensive?"

"N-no, I have the money." He rapped the tin bank. "But I wouldn't have enough to board him, not for six months. And anyway—"

"You've sort of lost your enthusiasm?" suggested Lucy.

"No, it's not that. I—I like Jerry." He blinked rapidly and cleared his throat. "If you saw Jerry, you might think I shouldn't have ever planned buying him. You might think he looks sort of—well, you might say oldish, and in six months he'll be that much older."

"We all will," Lucy said and gave a merry laugh.

"But, if you love Jerry—"

"Now, Lucy, when you see that B. B.'s trying to be adult about this—" Dave said, to be interrupted in turn by Tex.

"Hold on, Boss, I get Lucy's idea. We've got plenty of pasture, and there are a number of empty stalls in the old stable."

"And you owe it to B. B. after the way you treated him," Lucy said. "The least we can do is invite Jerry to visit us for the summer. What do you think of the plan, B. B.? It wouldn't cost you anything."

"We have plenty of room, and he'd be welcome," Dave said hospitably. "But if he's as old as George says, he might not live six months; then you'd be wasting your purchase price."

Brett knew he had but one thing to do: say right out that he had decided to spend the money on his mother. But instead he looked from speaker to speaker.

"Dave," Lucy spoke sharply, "you don't waste money when you spend it on a poor old animal who might be abused if anyone else bought him."

What she said was perfectly true. Brett felt as if he were being torn in two.

"Well, B. B., what do you say?" Lucy smiled as she asked the question.

Brett drew a deep breath and shook his head. "Thanks an awful lot, but I don't believe my father would let me board Jerry all that time for nothing."

"Yes, he will," Lucy said. "I'll phone him, and he'll understand how we feel. So that's out."

"But—but Jerry isn't exactly what you'd call a stylish horse."

"Then he'll make ours look all the handsomer," Dave said and smiled.

"There's still a lot to think about," temporized Brett. "Getting him here, for instance. Mr. De Luca's selling him any day now."

"When are you delivering that gelding, Tex?" asked Dave.

"Next week."

"Mind picking up Jerry?"

"I'd admire to."

Lucy clapped her hands. "Hurrah! It's all settled. Aren't you happy, B. B.?"

Brett stretched his lips in a forced smile. The time had come to either tell these people about the beater, or to say nothing and thank them.

"I—I had given up all idea of buying Jerry—but—but you're so kind, so generous! I can't thank you enough. It's too good to be true!"

The Hero

THE 8:10 local howled into the night's stillness; shaking the small station under the impact of its arrival. Only one passenger boarded the dimly lighted train.

"I'll give Jerry the best of care," promised Tex, standing by the steps.

"Thanks," Brett said soberly, then repeated with more enthusiasm, "Thanks a lot."

Brett waved from the platform, until the trainman beckoned him into the almost empty car. Sitting in a dingy red plush seat, he looked out the window and gazed at the reflection of the last person he wished to see—himself.

He'd never had much use for a guy who'd make a promise and break it. But now that the last obstacle had been cleared away, he could not give up Jerry.

Even his father shouldn't object. Although he didn't love horses, he'd certainly be glad that poor old Jerry was going to have a lovely home for six months.

Reaching the studio, Brett went immediately to bed, planning to get up when he heard his father's key

in the lock. He had a lot to tell him. But the first sound
he heard was the alarm clock next morning.

"Hi, Dad, I'm busting with news." He dropped
into the kitchen chair, uncertain how to begin.

"News, B. B.?" His father looked up from the
cornflakes he was shaking out. "You have me worried."

"This is good news, Dad." Brett found he wasn't
ready yet to tell his father about Jerry. That could wait.
"I know of a swell house we can buy cheap—"

"Hold on, Brett. Have you forgotten that we've
rented a house?"

"No, Dad, of course not. We can buy this when
our six months are up. It's near the station, just back of
the main street—only a few stores in the whole village."

"What village?"

"Ridgeview, Dad."

"Ridgeview? Isn't that where George has a home?"

"That's right. This house is a honey."

"How much?"

"Cheap, Dad. A real bargain."

"If it's such a bargain why hasn't it sold?"

Brett talked around a large mouthful of cornflakes.

"It isn't actually on the market yet. The Norths
are still living there, although they're moving very soon.
She'd like you to buy it because you're an artist and she
wants to be a painter herself."

His father got up to tend to the eggs. "Get to the
point," he said wearily. "I'm bored with the whole subject of houses."

Brett applied himself to his cereal before answering. He knew he could no longer evade the issue. "It's like this, Dad, the place used to belong to Dave's grandfather. He had a big farm, with lots of acres, but on one side the village bought some, and on the other there's a nice bunch of ranch houses. I even wish we'd taken one of them, Dad."

"Your bargain house doesn't sound very isolated, B. B."

"No, it isn't, Dad, but it's wonderful. It's shut in on one side by a row of trees and on the other by a wall of roses that are in full bloom." He paused, groping for courage, then he went on bravely, "So it really doesn't matter at all that the wall is really a wall of a movie house."

"Great guns, B. B., have we bumped into that movie house again?" Mr. Barnes slipped a soft-boiled egg into a holder and set it before Brett. "Better eat as you talk. Time's passing."

"But, Dad, wait'll you see it. They've invited us for lunch Saturday. You'll go, won't you? I said I thought you would. She's asking George, too. She'll telephone. You'll go, won't you, Dad?"

"I guess we can. But where'd you meet her, B. B.?"

"I had dinner with them last night. They eat in their kitchen. A big, lovely room."

"Whoa, B. B. Back up. You ate with these people in *their* kitchen up in *Ridgeview last night*?"

"That's right, Dad. It's a long story. I'll tell you about it at dinner. Not enough time now." That would give him a few hours in which to consider how he would present the subject of Jerry.

His father reached for the dangling crayon and crossed out the day with two broad strokes.

"Seventeen days left. Please don't do anything else crazy before your mother returns."

It wasn't crazy to buy Jerry. His father wanted him to own animals. Now if only he would buy the Norths' house, they'd be all set.

At school, however, he had plenty of time to tell George everything, and George made Brett repeat it to group after group who, in turn, told other boys. During lunch hour Brett was surrounded by eager questioners.

"Were you really a stowaway?"

"They thought *you* were a dead-end kid!"

"He actually had a real gun?"

"Is it true you're buying that old horse?"

The last question Brett always corrected before answering. "It isn't polite to call a person or a horse or any living thing old."

George had to leave as soon as school was out, but as he ran for his car Brett called, "If you hear from your uncle, tell him how grateful I am."

"You bet."

A small boy tugged at his arm. "Tell me about being kidnapped by gunmen. Please tell me."

Brett willingly plunged once more into his tale which had lost none of its excitement in the repetition. He enlarged on his dream and imitated the blowout with a mighty clap of his cupped palms.

"Hi, Brett, you're wanted," called one of the boys.

He looked around, conscious of a feeble auto horn.

It came from a junk car parked double.

At the wheel of the car sat Mr. De Luca.

Confessing

So Mr. De Luca had his auto, and at last Brett owned Jerry. It was something so big, so important, he couldn't take it in. How many boys in all the world owned a horse that they had paid for out of money they had earned?

"I'll tell you the rest of my tale tomorrow," he promised his small listener, and leaped to the junk car.

"Hello, Mr. De Luca, you certainly look elegant. Are you giving me a hitch?"

Mr. De Luca nodded, and Brett scrambled up beside him. He remembered what his mother had told him more than once. "Never be so happy yourself that you don't share another's happiness."

"This looks like a good strong auto, Mr. De Luca."

"Certainly it is-a strong. That is why I buy it."

"And you already know how to drive!"

"What good an auto if I no drive?"

Never a cheerful man, Mr. De Luca was unusually gloomy this afternoon. Brett thought he knew the reason, so he said with real sympathy, "I'm sorry if your friend is dead, Mr. De Luca."

"He ain't, not quite," answered Mr. De Luca, automatically reaching for a whip; then he returned his square hand to the wheel, and the auto jerked into motion. "Better tell you papa about the horse and get-a that settled."

"Oh, it is settled! Jerry's been promised a wonderful home in the country with nothing to do for the next six months but stroll around a pasture!"

"How you get him to this country?" scolded the owner.

"It's all arranged. They'll take him in their horse van. Know anyone who'd keep Jerry for a week or so?"

Mr. De Luca nodded grudgingly. "You give him, maybe $3?"

"Then everything's arranged, except for the wagon. Do you have any friend who'd like to borrow it for six months?"

"Lend—that is easy, but not always so good."

"Oh, I'd be glad to let someone use it; and I'll pay you everything today, if you'll drive around to my house."

"That can-a wait until you have told your papa and are ready to take him."

"But how can my father object? And I'm ready now, this minute! I would like to feel that I actually own him."

"You have-a made a down-paying, that is enough. Now, no more talk. I must pay attention. Driving a car, she is different from an old horse."

Brett cringed at the adjective, but sat in silence

until he was let off at Twenty-fourth Street.

Now he had only to tell his father, and that was a job he dreaded.

Whistling shrilly, he flung open the studio door and found his parent tied in an apron, at work on a Moorish lamp, transforming the black filagree into glittering brass.

"Hi, Dad, at work already!"

"Can't do everything the last minute, B. B."

"That's right, Dad. I'll yank on my working togs and help you." He started for the cubicle, but his father called him back.

"Just a second, son. Take time off and brief me as to what's what. Nobody tells me anything—or maybe I ought to say everyone's telling me a lot of stuff." He shook some metal polish onto his rag.

"Oh, that about me?" said Brett, dropping onto the piano bench.

"About you and a gang of gunmen and revolvers and what not." Mr. Barnes looked at his son with a serious gaze in which the usual twinkle was missing. "How come I'm the last to hear about it, B. B.?"

Brett twirled his cap on one finger. "I told you some. It's a long story, Dad. Talk about your happy endings! But it'll take a lot of time, which I spent this morning trying to make you buy the Norths' house, remember?"

"That's so," his father said. "Now you can have all the time there is, so shoot."

It didn't actually take Brett very long to complete

the tale of his adventure. He delayed telling about Dave's generous offer, but became enthusiastic about the luncheon invitation.

"Honest, Dad, I think when you see that house of theirs you'll be as enthusiastic as I am."

Mr. Barnes set the bottle down with a thump. "B. B., let's get this settled. If we get an invitation to visit these people in Ridgeview, I'll accept for your sake. On the other hand, for my sake, will you stop nagging about that house?"

"I will, Dad," Brett said so quietly his father softened his tone.

"Mind you, B. B., I'm no more enthusiastic over our rat-trap than you are; but we're taking it for your mother, and we'll have to hide our disgust. That's the least we can do."

"Sure, Dad. I'll remember."

"And there's another thing, B. B. Why did you want to see George's uncle?"

Brett sprang to his feet. "I've got something else to tell you, but I might as well be working at the same time."

When he returned he was given a pair of brass candlesticks that had never been polished since his mother went away.

"Well," said his father, "what else—"

"It's about Jerry, Dad."

"Jerry?" repeated his father.

"Yes, Mr. De Luca's horse."

"Oh, yes, Jerry. I'm amazed every Monday when

I hear his stumbling hoofs."

"You don't need to be, Dad. There's nothing the matter with his hoofs. The fact is, I've bought Jerry." Brett tried to express his pride of possession in his voice, but somehow he felt a wall of coldness between himself and his father.

"Not the peddler's old—" Mr. Barnes must have felt his son's hurt, for he did not finish his sentence.

"Yes, Dad. I told you. Jerry. Of course you can't appreciate him. I really believe you prefer dogs. Dogs are all right, but you can't compare them with horses! Mother would understand." He found the atmosphere so chilly he talked faster. "She'll be delighted to have me own Jerry. Maybe he isn't a thoroughbred, but he's the best I can afford, and he's alive! A real flesh and blood horse. And what's more, I have money enough to buy him."

"Does everybody know about your purchase, B. B., except your father?" Mr. Barnes asked quietly.

"Oh, no, Dad. Just George and the Norths and Tex and George's sister and maybe his father and mother . . ." The list did seem pretty long. "I wanted to surprise you, Dad."

"And didn't it ever occur to you that it might prove an unpleasant surprise?" asked his father.

"Yes, Dad, I guess I was a little worried."

"You had reason to be, for even if we had the prospect of a barn, I would not have allowed you to buy that horse. Have you paid for it?"

"Why not, Dad?" Brett asked, calmly ignoring the

question. "What's your reason?"

"I can think of two on the instant. One: He's too old. He may be sick any day and we could run up a big vet bill. Two: He might drop dead and then what do we do? How does one get rid of a dead horse?"

Brett shivered. "Dad, you're always looking on the dark side. Thank goodness the Norths don't feel that way. You don't have a worry. Everything's arranged. They've offered to board Jerry for six months. It won't cost a cent. They'll even drive him up in their horse van." Brett paused and bit his underlip in agitation, worried for the first time, lest his father refuse this generous offer.

"Why should they do so much for strangers?" Mr. Barnes asked sternly.

"Lucy said it was to make up for the way they'd treated me."

Suddenly the twinkle returned to Warner Barnes' eyes. "Brett, I don't think that's the real reason. I believe horse lovers are a clan. You understand each other. You like to do for each other—to play Santa Claus."

"Maybe, Dad, maybe. And you'll let David keep Jerry for me?" He waited, tense with worry, for his father's answer, realizing how much it meant to him. "Say, 'Yes', Dad. *Please* say 'Yes'."

"It's a big favor they're doing, B. B., and I'd like to pay something for his board, but I don't see how I can afford it." His father spoke thoughtfully as if he, too, suddenly wanted Brett to own Jerry.

"I don't think they need the money, Dad," Brett said, brushing aside the suggestion with a sweep of his hand.

"Suppose we shelve the question to be discussed Saturday if they invite us."

"Oh, they will, Dad. Lucy will. She said so. She'll be phoning any minute now."

"Don't be too confident, son." Mr. Barnes had gone back to his polishing. "People say things on the spur of the moment and change their minds afterward."

"But the Norths aren't like that, Dad," Brett said with conviction.

"We'll see, but even if they are able to keep Jerry, I'm afraid, B. B.," his father paused to shake more polish on his rag, "I'm afraid you're letting yourself in for a heartbreak. Whether you like it or not, Jerry is *old*."

"I know. That's why I'm glad he's going to have such a good home. You had me scared, Dad, that you wouldn't let the Norths keep him. Thanks an awful lot for not being like that."

Riding

Lucy North telephoned that evening, and Brett sat close enough to hear both sides of the conversation.

"I'm hoping," Lucy said, "you and your nice son can come for lunch Saturday, Mr. Barnes. We need to settle some details about Jerry, and I plan to sell you my husband's ancestral home."

Instead of sounding annoyed, as Brett feared he might, Mr. Barnes laughed.

"We'll be delighted to accept your invitation if it's understood that I'm not in the market for any house."

"Definitely," she agreed cheerfully. "But once you see the place, you won't be able to resist it."

"Want to bet?"

"Yes," she said laughing, "only I never bet on a sure thing."

When he had jotted down the route and rung off, he gave a little chuckle. "I suspect I'll like your friend, B. B."

"She's nice, Dad. They all are."

"Let me remind you that you, at least, have promised not to hound me about that house."

"That's right, Dad, but it is a lovely place."

"B. B., the Garden of Eden would lose its charm if it were next to a movie house. Don't, under any circumstances, get your hopes up, because I'm *not* buying it."

Brett repeated the conversation to George the next day.

"When you drive there Saturday, don't go past the movie house," George suggested. "Turn up the block before."

Brett nodded. "I get you. I wish Dad and I were going at night."

"He'd have to see it in the daytime sooner or later," George said wisely.

Nature seemed ready to back a hopeless cause, for in a year of days, none could have been more perfect than Saturday.

Brett was awakened by his father singing in a loud voice, "Oh, what a beautiful morning . . . !"

"It's wonderful, Brett, not to be hounding real estate offices," he said at breakfast. "Better wear your good blue suit and try to keep it presentable for our great reunion." He got up as he spoke and crossed out a day.

Brett found himself dreading a second view of the Norths' home; not that it made any difference, because his father wasn't buying it anyway. But even so he wanted it to live up to his praise.

They reached Ridgeview as the fire whistle announced the noon hour, which meant they were exactly on time.

"Turn up here, Dad," directed Brett. "And turn the next corner."

As they passed the new development he begged his father to go slowly. "Look at the nice ranch houses, Dad. See how they've put in trees and the streets aren't straight and ugly. See that line of pine trees? Our property would—I mean, the Norths' property begins there."

Brett was unprepared for the splash of rose buds that hung on the picket fence and brightened the wall of the movie theatre. The house, large and oblong, had been built with the narrow side to the road. There were flower beds gay with blooming May pinks, bleeding hearts, and late tulips. Why had he ever thought it would look better at night?

"I'm not saying anything about the house, Dad, but Mom would love those flowers."

"She would, indeed, B. B. But I'm saying something about the house. It needs painting; so does the barn."

"Stable, Dad. It used to be a big farm with a barn and stable and silo and all that stuff."

As his father turned in at the drive, Lucy flung open the front door and ran down the steps to greet them. She wore a swirling circular skirt, and slippers as red as the roses.

"It's so good of you to come, Mr. Barnes. I'm Lucy North." She held out her hand, not waiting for an introduction. "We've fallen hard for your son." And she slipped her left arm through Brett's. "Your father and I are having a contest, Brett. I say I'm going to sell him this house, and he says I'm not. Whom are you betting on?"

"My father, I'm afraid," Brett answered.

She and Mr. Barnes both laughed and he said, "I'm ready to admit the contest is more difficult than I anticipated."

"You mean you like it, Dad?"

"You said it was charming, Brett, and no one can deny it; but we've already rented a house, remember." He turned to his hostess. "We've had such a series of disappointments, B. B. and I, that I'm delighted to shelve the whole subject for the next six months."

"Let's do that," she agreed cheerfully. "How's Jerry, Brett?"

"Jerry's fine, I guess. I don't see him any more."

She led them to a terrace where the noon sun made it comfortably warm. "I invited you here a half hour early so I'd have time to show you the house; but since we've postponed the contest let's sit and get a tan."

To Brett's satisfaction, his father brought up the subject of Jerry again and expressed his gratitude at their generous offer. "You realize this buying of a junk man's horse is none of my doings."

Lucy laughed. "I doubt if an artist would appreciate Jerry."

"I think my mother will," Brett said. "And she's an artist, too."

"Your husband realizes, Mrs. North, that Jerry is burdened with many years?"

Brett glared at his father. Had he agreed to come

here only to spoil the deal? Nervously he awaited Lucy's reply.

"Naturally," she said. "That's to be expected. Tex wants to know, Brett, where he can pick up Jerry."

Brett breathed with relief. "I'll find out from Mr. De Luca on Monday. He never would tell me. I—I hope Jerry's had a nice stable, but sometimes I worry."

"Your worries will be over once he gets here."

"Oh, I know it," Brett said enthusiastically.

"I was wondering, Mrs. North," Mr. Barnes said changing the subject, "if you'd be willing to show me around the house I'm not going to buy?"

"Mind? I'd adore it." She jumped up and preceded them to the square front porch with its two shallow steps. Before entering the house she waved toward the lawn. "Room for tennis, badminton, or croquet. There's plenty of room beyond the stable for a vegetable garden."

As she led them from room to room, the double parlors, the library which they used as a bedroom, the large dining room, Brett's spirits sank. They were all furnished in ponderous walnut, upholstered in brown; the walls also were papered in brown. He could well imagine how his mother would hate it.

"We, being younger than Grandfather, never use the upstairs," Lucy explained. "But I can quickly whisk you around if you like. There are five bedrooms and another bath."

"No, don't bother," said Mr. Barnes; and Brett knew, even if he had been considering it, the whole deal would now be off. "Any restriction so one couldn't make this into two apartments?"

"Yes, there is," Lucy admitted regretfully. "They say the zoning'll soon be changed, and it would pay us to wait. But Dave wants to close the deal as soon as possible."

"That's understandable," Mr. Barnes turned and looked again at the gloomy rooms.

"Wait'll you see the kitchen," boasted Brett. "It's wonderful. Come on, let's show it to him." He pulled his father into the large cheery room, the round table set for six with a splashing centerpiece of spring flowers.

Despite the sunshine, the flowers, the yellow curtains, the rocking chairs, even this room did not look quite as wonderful as it had that night when he had come in stiff and frightened.

"Nice," his father said.

"It's where we live while we're camping out here," Lucy said. "As you can see, I haven't done anything with the other rooms. I tell Dave the house would sell more quickly empty."

"That might be," agreed Mr. Barnes, then added to Brett's complete surprise, "I like the place very much, Mrs. North, but even so, you don't win your bet, for I can't consider buying. Brett's mother, you know, has been very ill. I really think the small house we've rented is exactly what she ought to have, for the present, at any rate."

"I understand," Lucy said, her voice soft with sympathy. "But maybe at the end of six months—?"

"Maybe, if it isn't snapped up. But it will be."

So his father really liked it! Brett's hopeless yearning for the house felt like a hard knot in his heart, but he said, "I guess it *would* be too big for Mom."

A flash of red flickered across the kitchen windows, and Lucy flung open the door. "Here they are. Dave's brought George and Carol."

"Hi," called George, the first to enter. "How 'do, Mr. Barnes. What do you think of the place?"

"We like it," Brett said, answering for his father, "but it would be too much work for Mom."

It was a very pleasant meal. That was one thing about his father that Brett often noticed: everyone always seemed to be at ease with him; and when people were as nice and casual as the Norths, it was especially enjoyable.

While they were eating ice cream and angel cake, George asked as calmly as if it were not the most exciting question in the world, "Want to try some horseback this afternoon, Brett?"

"You mean that?" Brett looked from George to his sister, then across the table to his father. It had come as such a surprise he felt as if he ought to refuse. "We'll have to be getting home. Dad has a date. Haven't you, Dad?"

"You can make the city in an hour," encouraged Dave.

"But I haven't any clothes or—or anything," Brett said, wishing his voice didn't sound so shrill. Imagine actually riding a horse this very afternoon!

"There's old stuff in our locker," George said. "I'm supposed to exercise Dad's horse so you could take mine. He's as easy to ride as a hobby horse."

"Oh, it's not that I'm scared," explained Brett. "I'd love it, only—" He looked at his father questioningly.

"Could you stay until four, or four-thirty, Mr. Barnes?" Carol asked.

"Certainly. Suppose I said five, would that be all right?" Mr. Barnes looked at his son thoughtfully, as if he didn't understand why he hesitated.

"Then it's a deal," announced George. "Poor Brett'll wish he was dead long before that." And he gave his friend's arm an affectionate punch.

Sunnydale spread out over acres of level ground with innumerable yellow buildings: barns, paddocks, stables, an indoor ring. White fences outlined the outdoor riding ring and the various fields in which horses grazed. Brett could see it as they descended a hill, all laid out like a child's toy.

Dave turned Brett over to Tex, who greeted him and ordered a stable boy to harness George's horse and provide jodhpurs.

"How's Jerry?" Tex asked.

Brett smiled, his face alight with affection. "Jerry. Fine—I hope. The deal's all settled." He looked about him at all the sleek, well-cared-for animals. "I—I hope you won't be—be a little ashamed of him. He's really a wonderful—"

"Sure, I know he is," interrupted Tex. "Don't you

worry. He'll be treated like a star boarder. We'll pick him up Thursday."

"Thanks so much," Brett said and felt pure happiness envelop him.

Zipped into the borrowed jodhpurs, he found Carol leaning over a split rail fence waiting for him.

"A horse is a marvelous animal," she sighed reverently.

"You've said it," he agreed.

"Come on. Here's George's horse."

The next minute a bewildered Brett, acting under Carol's instruction, put his left foot in the stirrup and, after several efforts, flung his right leg over the back of George's small gentle mare.

It had happened! He, Brett Barnes, sat astride a living, breathing horse!

The Reckoning

THE following Monday Brett waited at the curb, a bag of carrots and lump sugar in one pocket, his tin bank in the other. Mr. De Luca must agree it was time to pay for Jerry.

The clank, clank of cow bells angered him. It wasn't fair for the auto to sound like the old junk cart. Also, Mr. De Luca's pride in his truck was disloyal. Jerry had served him faithfully.

"Hi, Mr. De Luca, how's my horse?" he called sternly.

The Prop ignored the question until he had weighed all the papers and paid for them.

"You ask-a, how is Jerry?"

Brett nodded. "I need his address. He's to be called for Thursday. Here's the money." He dug all the bills out of the tin bank and began to smooth them.

"Keep-a your money. You pay me nothings. You cannot have Jerry."

"But you can't *do* that. You sold him to me. You have a deposit." Brett's voice raised to a shout. "Even my father says it's all right."

Mr. De Luca gave one of his loose-jointed shrugs. "Your father say you can have him? He is wrong. Nobody on this earth can-a have Jerry."

"What do you mean?" A premonition chilled Brett's blood.

"Jerry—he is-a dead."

"No! Oh, no," begged Brett as if Mr. De Luca could do something about it. "He can't be. He was alive and well last Monday."

"He is not that now."

"When—when did he—"

"Last night, eight o'clock, nine o'clock."

Brett started to ask where he would be buried, but he had an awful feeling that Mr. De Luca had sold him to a glue factory, and he didn't want to know.

Mr. De Luca broke a long silence. "No need-a you feeling too sad. Jerry, he was-a very old. Your papa would not-a let you buy him."

"Oh, but he would," insisted Brett. "He would have loved to have me own him. So would my mother. And I had a wonderful place to keep him. Mr. De Luca, aren't you the least bit sorry he's dead?"

"Certainly I'm-a sorry. I lose a lot of money, but no horse can live forever."

"Was he sick—sick long?"

"Three days, four days."

Brett wondered if Mr. De Luca had had a vet. Had Brett known, he could have paid for at least one visit. It was too late now, too late to do anything. Jerry was dead. If only he could have lived long enough to get out to Ridgeview, they might have saved his life. Brett felt the bulging bag in his pocket and tears flooded his eyes. Poor Jerry.

" 'Bye, Mr. De Luca," he mumbled and started for his door.

"Come back," ordered the junk man so roughly that Brett blinked away the tears in surprise and obeyed. "How can I teach-a you to be a businessman? I owe you down payment."

Brett took the limp bills with a word of thanks, but he felt as if it were blood money. He didn't linger to watch the junk auto jangle along with the traffic. His paper business no longer meant anything to him. All his thoughts, his plans, his work had been toward the possession of Jerry, and Jerry was dead.

If only he could keep the hurt to himself and not tell anyone, not even his father or George. He had walked from habit up Second Avenue and along Twenty-fifth Street, and from habit he stopped in front of Harrison's. Looking through the glass at the stuffed horse, his mother's words came back to him. "Someday, Brett, you can own a palomino like that, or a roan, or a chestnut, or any kind of horse you'd like most—that is if you want it enough and will work for it."

How wrong she had been. Who had ever wanted a horse more than he, and hadn't he worked for him? Lugged tons of paper and modeled for hours? No, you didn't get what you wanted, but what was dished out to you, which was usually what you didn't want, like the nasty house in Jersey. Not that it made much difference where he lived, now that Jerry was dead.

George, waiting for him in front of the school, jog-trotted up to the corner to meet him.

"Hi, B. B., any news?"

"News?" Brett repeated and scowled.

"Yeh, about Saturday and the house. Any chance of your father changing his mind?"

"I told you there wasn't," he said peevishly. "He likes it, but it's too big for Mom, so forget it."

"All right, old Grouch, no need eating my head off."

During the reading period, Brett wrote a brief note to George: "Jerry is dead. Please make no remarks." This he sent across the room by the hand-to-hand method; and when George read it, he merely nodded.

Since this proved so satisfactory, he wrote a similar note to his father; and making a point of being home first, he stuck it to the face of the grandfather's clock; then taking his bank and the burned rug, he headed for the Armenian.

"I've brought the rug," he said, unrolling it. "Can you have it ready in a week?"

The Armenian shook his head.

"This is very much damaged. Like I told you before, it would not be worth the money." As he talked, he broke off the charred rim, making the hole twice as big.

"I know, but you said you'd do it for twenty dollars. You're not going back on your word, are you?"

With a shrug the man rolled up the rug and slid it toward Brett. His black eyes snapped and his voice, which had been soft and smooth, grew harsh. "I put in all my time. I make a beautiful, a perfect job—but you do not come for it. Your parents say it is too much money. So what happens? I am left with a little second-hand Bokhara rug that no one will buy for even fifteen dollars. It is impossible. When I said twenty dollars, I meant paid in advance, and that *you* will say is impossible."

"Oh, no, it isn't!" Brett gave a gasp of relief and took out his bank, from which he selected two of the four big bills. "Can you do it in a week, please?"

Instantly the man's thin face was wreathed in smiles and his manner became courtly.

"A week, I promise you." He picked up the bills. "When I have mended and washed it"—he gently laid the money in a drawer—"this will be a beautiful rug." He shut the drawer and bid the boy good afternoon.

Next, Brett decided to get the electric beater and settle that matter once and for all. Instead of going directly to Jake's and buying the one he had admired for months, he decided to check at a cut-rate store. With purposeful steps he climbed Murray Hill, dipped down to Forty-second Street and joined the bargain seekers in the electrical department.

There he saw the Acme beater just as new, just as glittering, as the one in Jake's window, at a reduction of $4.23.

As he trudged home with the heavy carton, he

actually whistled. For a short time, while he thought how pleased his mother would be when she received his gift, he forgot about Jerry.

How wonderful to have her back well and strong! She used to be so gay, so full of laughter. Surely his father *must* have missed her, too. Poor Dad, he'd felt hurt at not being told about Jerry. On an impulse, Brett decided to get him a reunion present, too.

Pausing to look into a drugstore window, he decided on a box of candy. His father loved chocolates. Inside, however, his eye was taken by the cigar counter. Cigars might be better; they wouldn't look as if he was buying something for himself.

"I'll take six of those," he ordered, then added a belated "please."

Fitted into a small bag they looked like nothing. Why, Brett asked himself, should he be so generous to his mother and so stingy to his father? After all, Jerry was dead and there was no other use for the money.

"A dollar," said the owner, holding out his hand.

"I've changed my mind, if it's all right," Brett said. "I've decided to buy that whole box of cigars, instead."

"It costs ten dollars," the owner said, staring at him through thick lenses. "Plus tax."

Brett gave him eleven dollars, pocketed the change, and strode home. He was mounting the steep stairs, lugging his gifts, when Mrs. McCray opened her door and called to him.

"I hear your mother's returning soon."

"Yes." He paused impatiently.

"A week from Thursday?"

"Yes, Mrs. McCray."

"I hope she isn't making a mistake, returning so soon."

"She's cured!" He planted his foot on the next step.

"That may be, but it can return. Someone told me you were moving to the country. Your father's very vague. Have you made any definite plans?"

"We've rented a house." He mounted the next step.

"Unfortunately we'll be away for a long week end when your mother returns, but I'll bring up a nice big lemon meringue pie before I go."

Mrs. McCray was always like that. When you knew you hated her for sure, she did something nice so you felt as if you ought to hate yourself.

He hid the Acme in the bottom of his closet and tucked the cigars in his middle bureau drawer. He heard his father enter the studio, heard him walk about. Then silence. He must be reading the note. Now he knew. Brett turned to face him.

"I'm clumsy at telling you I'm sorry, B. B.," his father said, standing in the doorway. "Too bad your mother isn't home. She'd know what to say. Although I'm glad the Norths were spared. I'm not going to say, 'Forget it,' but at the same time I hope you won't force yourself to brood over it. Know what I mean?"

"In a way, Dad."

"Jerry's dead and he's a great loss to you; but accepting a thing like that and carrying on, is part of growing up. I don't mean to sound too heartless."

"I'll be all right."

The next day George invited him to Ridgeview for the week end. Brett refused, saying he was busy helping his father fix up the studio. This was true enough, but not his real reason. He couldn't bear the thought of seeing all those happy horses in that lovely pasture.

As the days dragged by, Brett found that gradually he could think of Jerry without a choking, smothered feeling. But he couldn't look at a carrot or a lump of sugar.

Sunday evening, when he should have gone to the apartment next door to stack the newspapers in readiness for the morning, he picked up a book and dropped into a chair.

"I don't believe, Dad, I'll keep on selling papers."

"On account of Jerry, Brett?"

"That, and I don't need the money." As he spoke, he could see Jerry plodding up the street. "Seems sort of heartless."

"Does it? Seems to me sort of courageous. 'The king is dead, long live the king.' But it's up to you Brett. If you want, I'll carry on this once until the superintendent next door can get another boy."

Brett sighed and stood up.

"I'll do it, Dad."

The auto, its cowbells still jangling, awaited him

next morning as he came out with the last load.

"So you did-a come. Good." Mr. De Luca nodded his approval. "People live. People die. Work, she goes on. It is the same with animals. As for Jerry, *I* should be sad. *You* should be glad. You are lucky he die the week before, instead of the week after you buy him."

"Yes, that's right," agreed Brett. The very thought made his hands cold and sweaty.

"So, I see you next Monday?" Mr. De Luca asked when he had paid him.

"Yes," said Brett, wearily. "I suppose so."

"I know nothings about you no more. When you move-a, nothings," scolded Mr. De Luca. "Want I should pick you up after school tomorrow?"

"Why, yes, that would be nice," Brett said, wishing he could sound more enthusiastic. "Very nice."

"Then I come."

A G*ift*

B<small>RETT</small> paused on the stairs, letting the boys pass him like a rushing torrent, while he checked his brief case to make sure he had all the books he needed.

"Hi," George called to him from the front door, "your chariot's waiting for you."

"I know," answered Brett. "I'm coming."

He didn't really want to ride in Mr. De Luca's truck. He'd gone in it once to be polite, but beyond that was, it seemed to him, disloyal to Jerry.

"Sorry to keep you waiting, Mr. De Luca," he said, climbing in.

"I gotter more time to waste now I have an auto," Mr. De Luca said, rubbing salt into Brett's wound.

"Didn't you love Jerry at all?" Brett asked painfully.

Mr. De Luca said nothing until he shoved the clutch through all four gears. "Love? What-a you mean by love? He was a all right horse and me—I was a all right owner. I treat him good. Just the same you blame me that he die."

"Oh, no, Mr. De Luca, I don't *blame* you. I'm

sorry, that's all. Sorry you don't mourn him a little, just a little."

"I know, I know. You blame me because I don't mourn. Is that why you-a blame your father? Because he didn't mourn about your mama?"

A flush of guilt burned Brett's cheeks. "Why, Mr. De Luca, I never in my life said I blamed my father for anything. I love my father."

"Sure, sure. And why-a not? He a handsome, beeg, jolly man. He your papa, and a boy must love his papa. Just the same, you blame him. I know, not by what-a you say, but what-a you do not say. About your mama you talk all the time. About your papa—never."

"But my father's right here. I don't have to talk about him. My mother's three thousand miles away and—"

"Now you put your hand on it—or maybe should I say finger? Your mama is three thousand of miles away and you had-a to blame somebody, so you blame-a your papa. Jerry, he die, and you had-a to blame somebody, so you blame me."

Brett stared into space, his underjaw sagged, as he considered Mr. De Luca's statement.

"It's like-a child what trips over a chair and then pounds it with its leetle fist."

Mr. De Luca stopped at a red signal, and as if to show that he had closed the subject, took a half-burned cigarette from his pocket, picked off some lint, and lighted it at the risk of burning his lips.

"When you-a move to the country?" he asked in a

brisk tone.

Brett, glad to have his thoughts interrupted, said stiffly, "As soon as school closes, the tenth of June."

"And your mama come when?"

"In nine days."

"Without you-a telling me nothing, I know she is a very nice lady."

So he was trying to make up for calling him a leetle child. "Yes, she is," Brett said coldly.

"You-a ask me how I know?" Which was not the case. "I tell-a you. Because she have-a nice husband and she have-a nice son."

"But you just said I was a leetle child," protested Brett.

"Of course-a. You have been on this earth only a few years. Some old, old men is still leetle boys, but I think-a you will grow up."

"Thank you," Brett said, comforted by the sincerity of Mr. De Luca's praise. "I guess I sort of know what you mean."

"I have a present for you back there." Mr. De Luca tossed away the butt and jerked his head. "Look-a and see."

Brett turned and studied the merchandise: newspapers, an old bedspring, two broken chairs, and a wooden table. Close to the seat lay a machine with a long handle, partly covered by some rags.

"Is it this?" Brett asked, pointing a thumb.

"Right. It's a roto-go-round grass cutter machine."

"Oh! Oh, how wonderful! I've only seen pictures

of them." Excitement brightened Brett's eyes.

"Me neither," agreed Mr. De Luca. "Nobody needs them in the city. But in-a the country you can go into business. Get-a yourself customers."

"Of course I can. We won't have much grass ourselves, I suppose, because we're renting a little house, so I'll have plenty of time to cut other people's lawns. And even if it's broken, my father's smart about fixing machinery."

"It is-a *not* broke. Not now. Me—I-a am smart with machines, too. I fix it. I clean it. I oil it. I paint it. Now it is-a perfect."

"Well, it's a wonderful, wonderful present, Mr. De Luca. I know my father will want to thank you personally. And so will my mother when she gets here."

"It's not-a so much," Mr. De Luca said modestly.

"It's the biggest present I ever got in my whole life."

Instead of letting Brett out at the corner, Mr. De Luca drove up to the door of the studio and together they lugged out the heavy electric mower.

"Best I should-a help you up the stairs," Mr. De Luca insisted. Setting the machine down in the upper hall, he would not go into the studio. "Want I should get a ticket?"

"I can't thank you enough, Mr. De Luca." Brett gazed admiringly at the gift. "It looks brand new with that green enamel."

"Me, I'm not such a good painter as your papa, but it hides scratches. And it will cut grass, that I know.

I think, mebby, with that whirl-around machine you can-a have business even in the country."

"Of course I can, Mr. De Luca. It'll be a cinch to cut acres of grass."

"And with a machine like that you should-a get more pay. And with more pay you will be able to save money and some-a day you can buy a real horse."

Brett flinched at the word real. "Yes, someday, maybe, but I don't think I'd want a horse, even a young horse right away. You see, Mr. De Luca, Jerry was very real to me."

"I know how-a you feel. That is, how-a you think you feel; but if-a you had a chance, I think you change your mind-a pretty quick." He gave a throaty chuckle. "Want-a I should stop again if ever I pass the school?"

"Yes, please. Any day—every day—but remember, on Fridays we get out at two-thirty."

Mr. De Luca stumped down the stairs muttering, "Listen to him, as if-a I had nothings else to do."

Understanding

THE power mower made a great hit with Mr. Barnes. He suggested that they pay Mr. De Luca, who had already suffered a financial loss with the death of Jerry, but Brett felt sure Mr. De Luca wanted it to be a gift.

Day followed day with leaden slowness. Mrs. Barnes wrote that she couldn't wait to see the little house they had rented and it was quite all right for her to live in the city until the middle of June. "You foolish worry-pots," she wrote, "don't you realize I'm cured!"

Brett, no longer saving every cent, treated George to a soda on Monday, using the money he had made on papers that morning. It was then he learned that Uncle Dave and Aunt Lucy would be moving into their new house the next day.

"And they've sold their old place?" Brett asked.

George nodded. "Gee, your father missed a swell bargain."

"I told you—"

"Sure, I know, but any house is *work*. No house

keeps itself." George sucked up the last of his soda with a noisy gurgle.

"I'm not saying anything yet, George, but I'm hoping my parents will buy one of the ranch houses next to that property. They don't look so bad."

George agreed that they might be worse, and the two boys dreamed about the fun they would have if the Barneses would move to Ridgeview.

Wednesday night Mr. Barnes drew the last red cross on the calendar, and they both set their alarms for five A.M.

"We have to have plenty of time to do this right," Mr. Barnes said.

"Sure," agreed Brett, knowing he would be awake before the alarm went off.

The plane was due in Idlewild at 4:30 P.M. Both Brett and his father had permission to leave school at 2:00 P.M. and, regardless of expense, they hopped a taxi to the studio. While his father stopped to buy flowers, Brett hurried on ahead. He was halted halfway up the stairs by Mrs. McCray who exhibited the promised pie with its mountain of meringue.

"I'll carry it," she said and followed him. Brett unlocked the door and she stood blocking the way as she gazed about her. "I knew you'd had Mrs. Haggerty every day this week, but I didn't suppose anyone could perform such a miracle!"

"Thank you," Brett said, not sure whether it was a compliment or an insult. "Guess we weren't very good housekeepers, Dad and I."

"I wouldn't say that at all, not at all," she scolded, striding to the kitchen. "You should be proud of yourselves, the way you've managed, you two. I'll set the pie on top of the refrigerator—even your kitchen looks spotless—then I'll have to hurry. We're leaving in an hour—for the whole week end, you know. I'm so sorry not to be here to greet your mother."

"I know," Brett said, and shut the door after her; then remembering he had not thanked her, opened it again.

"Thanks a million for the pie, Mrs. McCray. Mom'll love it—we all will."

"I hope it's good. Tell your mother I'll see her Monday."

Alone again, he hurried into his white Sunday shirt and his best suit. Borrowing some of his father's pomade, with the aid of military brushes, he slicked back his hair so that it made an arrow over his forehead. He studied his reflection in the mirror wondering if he would look any different to his mother. Certainly his hair was darker. According to the school record he had grown two and a half inches and gained six pounds, but it seemed to him his face was skinnier. He parted his lips and looked at his chipped front tooth.

"Hi, B. B.," called his father, and shut the door with his foot. "Want to help an overloaded mule?"

Together they put away the groceries while Mr. Barnes praised the pie and detailed to Brett what he had bought for dinner. "It's the bride's special: lamb chops, frozen French fries, frozen peas, lettuce with garlic dressing, and that elegant pie topped off with cheese. We'll show your mother we know our way around."

Brett grinned.

When Mr. Barnes had arranged a vase of snapdragons and lilacs, he set it on the piano, careful to drip no water. "Place does look nice," he called to his son.

"That's what Mrs. McCray said. Guess it's time to put down the rug, eh, Dad?" Brett cut the cord and spread it in front of his mother's couch.

"That's the crowning glory, B. B. So white, so red, so beautiful! A truly generous home-coming present."

"Generous nothing, Dad. I burned it. But I do have a real present for Mom. A—a sort of egg beater." He didn't want his father to know how really important it was. "And I have something for you, too. A stay-at-home present."

"For *me*? Well, now, what do you know? Maybe this is the time to tell you, B. B., as I've written to your mother often enough, I'm proud of the way you've stood up to the separation. I know it wasn't easy."

"Oh, it wasn't so bad," Brett said, blinking rapidly, as he dashed into the cubicle.

His father seemed stunned by his gift. "A box, B. B.? A whole box? I never had so many cigars at one time in my life!"

"You deserve it, Dad. You haven't been such a bad father, either."

Mr. Barnes stood for a moment looking at the gift, then he raised his eyes to his son's. "I guess maybe we've turned the corner, B. B., and caught up with our good luck."

"I hope so, Dad. I sure hope so," Brett said.

"About tomorrow, B. B. I've arranged to have the day off. Want to take your mother out to see the house we've rented. How about you? Maybe you ought to go to school."

"Sure, Dad. It isn't as if we were buying the house."

His father changed into his best suit and left nothing about. "Ready, B. B.? We ought to get off."

"O.K., Dad. I'll get my jacket." As he slipped his coat from the hanger, he gently kicked the Acme carton. He'd kept his vow, finally, hadn't he?

The old Buick got them to Idlewild in less time than they had estimated, which was fortunate as the flight, helped by a tail wind, was ahead of schedule.

As they stood with the group of eager welcomers, Brett's heart seemed to have lost its moorings. He held himself together by interlocking his fingers and pressing his arms into his ribs.

A loud speaker crackled, "Flight 452 from Rome, Paris, London, Shannon, now landing."

In the far distance Brett saw the glitter of a silver gnat. Then it grew into a sea gull and finally a sun-sparkled plane! It swirled over the field, took the wind head on, and dipped earthward.

He pressed his arms tighter against his body.

There it was skimming along the runway. It slowed down and came bumping toward him until it was so close he could see the oil-stained aluminum. Then it stopped.

Brett drew a deep breath and leaned forward as the steps were rolled up to the plane. The door swung open. A hostess stepped onto the platform. He squeezed his stomach tighter.

A man came out with a brief case. He and the hostess nodded to each other. Another man. A third man. A fat woman—his mother had gained weight, but surely not that much. He saw that his father was not interested in her. There were more men, then an old woman who was helped down by the hostess. Was she old or was she sick? Could his mother be—no, the woman really was old and white haired. More men. A woman who could be—who might be—again he sought his father's face and saw no light of recognition.

More men, then a girl in a plaid suit, carrying a round hat box. A movie star; they always carried hat boxes. For a silly moment he wondered if it could possibly be his mother, but this woman had short curls blowing about her small hat, and his mother had long hair. He remembered the braids on either side of her thin neck when she lay in bed.

His father nudged him, and shouted, "Lee! Hi, Lee!"

The girl, the movie star, pulled off her tam-o' shanter and waved. Then he could see it was his mother.

His throat contracted. An uncontrollable sob escaped. He pulled out the handkerchief he had folded so carefully, and bending over, covered his streaming eyes. As he cried, his shoulders shook. Now and then a sob escaped.

Blindly, feeling his way with his feet, he escaped from his father and hid behind a post.

He felt a hand on his arm. "Brett," his father said.

"I—I can't help it, Dad. I'll be all right, by the time she's through customs."

"Look at me, B. B." Obeying, unwillingly, he saw that his father's face was also streaked with tears. "That's how it is, B. B.—even with men—when they really care."

Brett nodded, and suddenly a smile changed his whole expression. How wrong he'd been all these months. He had a wonderful father. Without any "buts" and "ifs" he had a swell father.

The Promise

THEY all three crowded into the narrow front seat. As Brett felt his mother's arm about him, smelled a strangely familiar fragrance, and listened to her clear English pronunciation, he wondered how he had lived without her.

They talked about the flight, about English food, and English weather, unimportant things that had to be gone over.

"Lee, you can be proud of the way you raised your son," Mr. Barnes said as they sped down the drive. "I wasn't exaggerating in my letters. He's grown into quite a man."

Brett's cheeks felt hot as his mother said, squeezing his shoulder, "I know, Warner. They don't come any better."

"Aw, you're both crazy," he muttered, and hurriedly changed the subject.

"Looks familiar," she said as the car turned down Twenty-fourth Street. "If it weren't for Brett having a real room of his own, I'd say, why move?"

"Don't worry about me, Mom. I'm not so crazy to have a real room."

"That's because you've never had one. You'll change your mind."

Mr. Barnes drew up at their door. "Get out the suitcases, B. B., and make your mother a cup of tea. English ladies can't live without their afternoon tea." He kissed his wife lingeringly. "Now, if only I can find a parking place."

Mrs. Barnes stood looking after the ancient high-built auto. "How fortunate we are, Brett, having a man like your father."

"You said it, Mom," Brett agreed with enthusiasm.

"The McCrays," his mother whispered as he followed her up the stairs. "Still here?"

"Sure—but away for a long week end. She made you a pie."

Mrs. Barnes nodded contentedly. "She's a good woman—but. Brett, let's go in the studio together."

"Wait'll I get your other suitcase." He set down the two he carried and went for the third.

As he unlocked the door, she said in a whisper, "I feel as if I were entering heaven," and held out her hand like a child.

He felt her fingers tighten on his as he kicked open the door.

"Oh, Brett, how beautiful! I tried to dream about it every night and I often did, but it looks even better than my best dreams." She let go of his hand and wandered about. At the couch she stopped.

"Brett! My Bokhara rug! It looks new!"

"Yeah, it does. The man washed it after he mended it. I didn't tell you, Mom, but I burned a hole in the center."

"Doesn't show. It couldn't have been big."

"Sure was, but I had it woven."

"I suppose there're a lot of things I never was told," she said soberly, then gave one of her merry little laughs. "But if you'd told me forever what wonderful housekeepers you two are, I never would have believed you."

Brett gave a broad grin. "Mrs. Haggerty did some extra work, and so did we."

"You must have. Oh, Brett, what did I ever do to deserve the best husband and the best son in all the world?"

Brett shrugged off his share and said, "You're not such a punk mother yourself, you know."

"I've been a total loss for the last year. It's a wonder you can even remember when I was any good. But that's history, and we're facing the future."

"And I have to make some tea," Brett reminded her.

"Not for me, darling. I want to get busy with our dinner. How I've longed to get back into harness."

"I don't believe Dad'll let you tonight, Mom. He has everything arranged." Ever since the car drew up at the door, Brett's mind had been skirting around the Acme. "Mom, I have a home-coming present for you. I've already given Dad a staying-home present. Suppose

I get yours?"

"How exciting! Yes, do get it, and don't walk—run."

He dashed into his cubicle and returned in a flash with the carton which he set on the tea table.

"Now what on earth," murmured Mrs. Barnes, sitting on the couch and turning her head sideways to read the lettering on the carton. "It says Acme Beater, but of course it can't be that. Remember, when you used to do all the beating for me, we'd talk about getting one some day."

"Sure I remember. Here, Mom, let me—" He sliced the gummed paper with a letter opener and opened up the top.

His mother stood up to peer inside the box. "Brett, it isn't—it can't be—Brett Barnes, it *is*!"

Standing motionless, she watched him draw out the white enameled stand, the blades, the two bowls, the juicer. It did look quite splendid.

"Brett, it's—it's magnificent!"

For a second he wanted to tell her how near she had come to not getting it; but she was impatient to see it work, and he let the opportunity slip by.

When Mr. Barnes came in, the Acme was shirrling madly on the piano bench.

"Say, B. B., that really is a present!" he exclaimed.

"I told you about it, Dad," Brett said guiltily, remembering his misleading description.

"Yes, I know, but I thought it was a dinky little hand affair. Lee, our prosperous son gave me a fabulous present, too. Hold on a second."

Proudly he exhibited his box of cigars, and his wife turned off the beater to admire them.

"Sorry I can't share them, Lee. I hate to seem stingy with such a generous son."

"Generous, nothing," growled Brett. "You really ought to thank Jerry. When I thought I was in a gunman's car—"

"A *gunman's* car, Brett? When was that?"

"It was really Mr. North, Mom, but I thought he was a killer." Brett paused, finding it hard to make his confession. "I vowed to myself, if I got out alive, I'd forget about poor Jerry and buy the Acme instead. I'd planned to give it to you the day you left. But did I keep my promise? No. Instead he had to die. So you see, I'm really just a stinker."

"Darling, you're just human," his mother said gently. "Maybe that's the trouble with the world. We all make vows we don't keep. Isn't that so, Warner?"

"I'm afraid you're right, Lee. But I know one thing. I know that Brett's confession just now took— pardon the expression, Lee—took guts. I'm proud of B. B."

"Include me in that, Brett, and lend me a hand," his mother said, jumping up. "I brought a few little gifts myself, if you'll unstrap that small suitcase while I get the key."

She had brought them Irish linen handkerchiefs, English jackknives and Scotch bathrobes. Brett's was the bright red Royal Stuart tartan, his father's the green

Hunting Stuart.

"Like Christmas," his father said, tying on his bath-robe. "Well, I'm not caught entirely off guard. I have nothing for you, Brett, I'm sorry to say; but I've a wee gift for our new housekeeper." He swaggered over to his chest of drawers, returning with a small box which he dropped into his wife's lap.

When she took out a diamond-horseshoe pin, surrounded by a heart-shaped wreath of gold leaves, her surprise and admiration were no greater than Brett's.

"Warner Barnes! Have you struck oil?"

"To a lesser degree, oil paint," he said and made no effort to hide his pleasure. "Glad you like it."

"But, Dad, are the diamonds *real*?" questioned Brett.

"Sure they're real. Recognize my father's old scarf-pin, Lee?"

"And you had the laurel wreath added. Oh, Warner, I feel frightfully selfish."

"Nonsense. Scarf-pins are out."

"But they'll come in again."

"In any case, I can see it better on you. Come on, B. B., we have a job to do." He pointed toward the kitchen. "And no butting in on your part, my fine lady."

"I told you so, Mom," Brett said and pridefully followed his father.

Homecoming

BRETT lay in bed enjoying a new sense of bliss, a feeling of completeness.

The clink of china and his parents' low voices reached him in his cubicle, together with the spicy odor of frying sausages. Their traditional Sunday breakfast: waffles and sausages, and this was only Friday.

Five minutes later he presented himself, completely dressed, hair parted and dripping wet. A new yellow cloth covered the refectory table and a small vase held a few lilacs.

"Morning, Mom and Dad. Where'd the table-cloth come from?"

"Brett, how nice you noticed! It's a studio present from Shannon. And speaking of presents—I made the waffle mix in the beater and was it wonderful! Sit down, dear. You, too, Warner. Everything's ready."

"Not bad, having a resident cook, eh, B. B.," joked Mr. Barnes.

"And such a contented cook," added his wife.

Brett's whole day was colored by his mother's return. She sent him off with the promise that they'd be back from Jersey by the time he returned from school. Even the thought of the rented house failed to dim his spirits.

Before school started, he showed George his new knife. "Best steel in the whole world, named after you, I. X. L. George. And you ought to see my mother. Bet she never looked weller—more well—in her whole life."

"It's like I said. She could have taken care of Uncle Dave's house." George sounded annoyed at the good news.

"Maybe she could have," Brett agreed cheerfully. "But the important thing is, *she's well*."

It was Friday and school was over at two-thirty. At the electric click, before the buzz, Brett was out of his classroom, just as he used to be when Jerry came for him.

To his surprise, Mr. De Luca's truck was parked double right in front of the school and beside it stood his father and mother chatting with the Prop himself.

"Hi, B. B.," called his father, waving his hat.

Brett joined them and his mother slipped her hand through his arm. "We've had a nice visit with your friend, Brett, and we've told him how much we appreciate that power mower."

"I hope-a it has more life in it than poor old Jerry," Mr. De Luca said gloomily, then his tone brightened. "Now-a I can see I was-a right. You both are two reasons why-a your boy is-a a nice boy."

"Mr. De Luca," gasped Brett's mother, "that's the

loveliest compliment we three ever had."

Mr. De Luca played a little tune with his fingers on the steering wheel to show his unconcern. "I tell-a what is true," he said and started the engine with a mighty roar.

"You came to give me a hitch, Mr. De Luca?" Brett shouted above the noise, not knowing what he should do.

Throttling the engine, Mr. De Luca nodded and said, "But-a your papa and mama want you; so I go." And living up to his word he started off with a jerk.

"See you Monday," called Brett, and turned to his parents. "What brought you here, Dad?"

"You. Come along, get into the car. We have a lot
to tell you." His father headed for the big old Buick
halfway down the block, but Brett grabbed his mother's
arm and dragged her in the other direction.

"There's George, Mom. You know, my best friend
—came to Cluett last fall." He raised his voice and
shouted, "Hi-ya, George, come here."

George obeyed on a gallop, stopped short in front
of Mrs. Barnes, and gazed at her in wide-eyed admiration.

"My mother, George."

"It's grand to see you, Mrs. Barnes. B. B.'s been
always talking about you, and I don't wonder."

"He's been always writing about you, George, and
I don't wonder either." She gave one of her little,
musical laughs. "We must have a get-together, but now
we'll have to get going. As you can see, my husband's
having a fit."

In a maze of confusion, Brett scrambled into the
front seat beside his father and squeezed himself together to make room for his mother.

"What's all the excitement, Dad? I don't get it."

"We're taking your mother to see the house."

"Haven't you been yet?"

"No, dear, not yet," his mother said. "I had to unpack and it was such bliss to be home and we had so
much to talk about. Anyway, it's more fun to have you
along. I'm positive I'll love it. Your father sent me a
picture." She looked over his head and spoke to his
father. "Oh, Warner, darling, let's not tease the boy."

Brett squeezed his face into puzzled wrinkles and looked from one parent to the other. Tease him? What did she mean?

"I'm not teasing, Lee," his father answered. "I'm protecting the kid from further disappointments. It's a matter of vital interest to you, and you're not going into it blindly. If I sound cryptic, B. B., I'll explain everything in a little while."

"Darling, your father loves surprises more than I do. But this is his project, and we'll play along with him. Please, dear, give me a blow by blow description of the time you thought you were in a gunman's car."

Willingly Brett repeated the story and delighted in his mother's reaction.

"Oh, darling, what a terrible experience. Now tell me about Mr. De Luca. He's such a delightful character."

"Nothing much to tell, Mom, except he's my friend. Say, Dad, haven't you passed the George Washington Bridge?"

"Yes, I'm heading for Ridgeview first—want to see the Norths—then we can take the Tappanzee Bridge. Makes a nicer ride."

"And your friend, George, Brett," continued his mother. "He seems very nice."

"Sure, he's a good egg, only he's awful mad that we didn't buy—" Suddenly he remembered his promise. Probably his mother didn't even know about that house. "He's mad we don't buy in Ridgeview. They have some nice ranch houses there, Mom."

When they reached the tiny village of Ridgeview, Brett sat forward in his seat fascinated by the familiar scene.

"This is the movie theatre, Lee," his father said like an announcer on a sight-seeing bus.

"It's a nice looking building," praised his mother, "and a cute little town."

"Yes," agreed Brett.

His father turned right off Main Street and right again, which took them past the North's vacant home. Brett sat back and eyed it stonily. It was his mother who now leaned forward.

"Warner! It's *charming*! All those flowers! Much,

much better than your picture. I don't mind the wall at all. I *know* I want it." She wrapped Brett in a tight embrace. "Brett, darling, your father's buying it! He is, he is!"

"He can't," lamented Brett in sudden anguish. "He's too late. It's been sold."

Ignoring his son's lament, Mr. Barnes drove up to the kitchen door.

"I tell you, Dad, it's sold. George said so."

"That's right, B. B. It's sold to me. That is, the North's are holding it until your mother sees it."

"Aren't we the luckiest family, Brett!" his mother exclaimed. "No wonder you wanted it. Not in a hundred

years did I suppose we'd own anything like it."

Still in a state of complete confusion, Brett got out of the car and watched his parents search for a key hanging on a lilac bush.

"Here it is," said his father. "Come on, Brett, we have to show your mother around."

"But, Dad, you've already paid a binder on that awful—"

"I know. I'll phone her tonight. She doesn't really want a boy your age, and I think she'll be glad to get out from under.

"B. B., don't look as if you'd seen a ghost," begged his father. "I didn't tell you because I thought you'd had enough disappointments; but that day we were here for lunch, I told Lucy North I'd buy the place, furniture and all, if your mother liked it. Now will you please lead the way."

Dutifully, Brett preceded his parents from room to room, while his mother raved about everything. When, at last, they had made a complete circuit and returned to the kitchen which had been left intact, Mrs. Barnes sank into the rocking chair and said in an awed tone, "To think that we're getting all this furniture! When I've made bright slip covers you won't know it; and, Warner, when you and Brett have painted and papered the walls, it'll be a *beautiful* house. Oh, I can't believe it's ours, can you, Brett?"

"No," he said.

"Darling, I brought what's left of the lemon meringue pie in a hat box in the back of the car. Will you get it carefully? We'll have it with a cup of tea. Maybe it'll make us feel at home."

Home, Brett repeated to himself as he did as she requested, this is to be my home. I'll live here, I'll go to school here, and maybe some day I'll even work at the Sunnydale Riding Academy.

While they were having pie and tea at the round table, Warner Barnes telephoned to Mrs. North and told her he was ready to give her a check. "That is, if my wife doesn't float away on a pink cloud," he said with a laugh. Then he said, "Thanks a lot, Lucy, but not tonight. We're going to have a delicatessen supper right here under our own vine and fig tree. Yes, we're staying until Sunday afternoon. Thanks for suggesting it."

"We'll be here *all night*?" queried Brett, in an undertone while his father told Lucy how much they loved the place.

His mother nodded and whispered, "Lucy phoned this morning and invited us. I have blankets, sheets, and clothes for us in the luggage compartment. We'll probably be coming every week end."

"Oh," said Brett, then in a gay tone, "oh, good. Swell! Maybe I can call up George, later on, and tell him the good news."

"Of course you can." His mother refilled her cup. "Such a darling old teapot."

Warner Barnes rang off and said he'd refused a dinner invitation and made an eleven o'clock date at the lawyers Saturday morning to sign the contract.

"How come you haven't taken a look at the stable,
B. B.?" he asked in a manner that seemed to Brett very
self-conscious.

It gave the boy an idea. Everything seemed to be
happening today. What if there might be a horse waiting for him in the stable! The thought sent his heart
rocketing. He had told Mr. De Luca he didn't want a
horse for a long time, but if there should be one—

"Wait for me," begged Mrs. Barnes, hurriedly
drinking her tea. "I love stables, too."

"Must be an honest village," Mr. Barnes said,
flinging open the unlocked double-doors.

Did that mean there was something inside worth
stealing? Brett freed himself from his mother's arm,
lest she feel his pounding heart, and stepped over the
worn sill. A quick glance along the four stalls told him
how crazy he had been. They were empty.

"Look, Brett, at all they've left," his mother said
excitedly. "That's a nice one-seater. What do they call
it? A trap? And a little old wagon, and a saddle and a
bridle—all yours, Brett, she said so."

"And here's quite a decent whip." Brett's enthusiasm was forced for he couldn't help wishing poor old
Jerry occupied one of those stalls.

"What you need now, B. B., is a horse," his father
said, and he didn't sound as if he were joking.

"That's right, Dad," Brett said, flashing his father
a smile of appreciation. "When we get the house fixed
up, I'll earn money cutting lawns. That's why Mr. De
Luca gave me the power mower."

"I hate to disappoint Mr. De Luca, B. B., but *I'm* going to work for your horse." His father didn't seem to be joking. "The idea pleases me. It'll be good for my soul—me a dog lover."

"You're fooling, Dad?"

"I am not. Dave North made the suggestion, and it's a fair barter. He'll swap a horse for a portrait of his wife."

"And you'd do that for me, Dad? Is he serious, Mom?"

"I'm sure he is."

"Never more so, B. B. I owe you a reunion present."

"Gee, Dad." Brett looked up at his father, his eyes aglitter.

"How can I ever thank you enough? Say, Mom, is there any danger of a guy being too happy?"